Perfect Wedding

A Comedy in Two Acts

Robin Hawdon

A SAMUEL FRENCH ACTING EDITION

FOUNDED 1830

SAMUELFRENCH.COM
SAMUELFRENCH-LONDON.CO.UK

FOR PRODUCTION ENQUIRIES

UNITED STATES AND CANADA
Info@SamuelFrench.com
1-866-598-8449

UNITED KINGDOM AND EUROPE
Theatre@SamuelFrench-London.co.uk
020-7255-4302

Each title is subject to availability from Samuel French, depending upon
country of performance. Please be aware that *PERFECT WEDDING* may
not be licensed by Samuel French in your territory. Professional and
amateur producers should contact the nearest Samuel French office or
licensing partner to verify availability.

MUSIC USE NOTE

Licensees are solely responsible for obtaining formal written permission from copyright owners to use copyrighted music in the performance of this play and are strongly cautioned to do so. If no such permission is obtained by the licensee, then the licensee must use only original music that the licensee owns and controls. Licensees are solely responsible and liable for all music clearances and shall indemnify the copyright owners of the play(s) and their licensing agent, Samuel French, against any costs, expenses, losses and liabilities arising from the use of music by licensees. Please contact the appropriate music licensing authority in your territory for the rights to any incidental music.

IMPORTANT BILLING AND CREDIT REQUIREMENTS

If you have obtained performance rights to this title, please refer to your licensing agreement for important billing and credit requirements.

Our 63rd Season   *August 19 thru August 31*

PENINSULA PLAYERS
theatre in a garden

James B. McKenzie, Executive Producer

presents

Perfect Wedding

by Robin Hawdon

featuring
(in alphabetical order)
McKinley Carter, Steve Hinger°, Alan Kopischke°, Leisa Mather°,
Bradley Mott°, Susan Osborne-Mott°, and Julie Pearl

Directed by Amy McKenzie

° Indicates performers and stage managers who are members of Actors' Equity Association,
the union of Professional Actors and Stage Managers.

Production Stage Manager - Kevin Casey°
Assistant Stage Manager - Jennifer Barclay
Scenic Designer - Betsy Leonard
Costume Designer - Kärin Simonson Kopischke
Properties/Sound Designer - Galen Ramsey
Lighting Designer - Steve White

This play is supported in part by the Wisconsin Arts Board
with funds from the State of Wisconsin.

CHARACTERS

RACHEL, the bride (20s, always in command)
BILL, the groom (20s, rarely in command)
TOM, the best man (20s, solid, dependable)
JUDY, a girl (20s, very attractive)
JULIE, a chambermaid (20s, kooky, volatile)
DAPHNE, the bride's mother (40s, emotional)

NOTE: This published text has the play's original English setting. However producers in the U.S.A. may wish to relocate the play in America, as has been done with a number of professional productions. This simply entails changing the odd place name (i.e. New York/Los Angeles for London), and altering any specifically English phraseology. The author has no objection to this.

SETTING

The honeymoon suite of a gracious period country-house hotel somewhere in the country outside London. Traditional chintz, William Morris, antiques and framed rural prints. We can see the two main rooms. Stage right the reception room. A sofa is the main piece of furniture. A large bay window in the right hand wall gives a glimpse of a village green and church. Upstage a door to the passage. Center stage a token 'wall' with a connection door in the upstage portion which leads to the bedroom. An ornate double bed upstage left, facing downstage, possibly at an angle. A dressing table to the left of it. Another passage door upstage to the right of the bed, mirroring the one in the reception room. A door downstage left to an off-stage en-suite bathroom. Sunshine, birdsong, and traditional English village sounds.

PERFECT WEDDING

ACT I

(Morning. BILL lies asleep in the double bed. He stirs, awakes gradually, groans, and sits up. He looks awful. As his senses return he frowns blearily round, trying to remember where he is. Becomes aware of a hump under the duvet. Prods it speculatively. It murmurs and moves. He recoils in astonishment. Cautiously lifts the edge of the duvet and peers under. Hastily replaces it and thinks frantically.)

BILL. Oh, God! *(Pause.)* Oh my God! *(Pause.)* Oh my God!

(Steals another look. The figure stirs again, and a tousled female head appears form under the duvet. It peers sleepily round, then sees BILL.)

GIRL. Hello.
BILL. Who are you?
GIRL. Oh, charming. Thanks.
BILL. Do I know you?
GIRL. That's really nice. That's very flattering.
BILL. I'm very sorry, but I... *(Holds his head.)* it's my head.
GIRL. What's wrong with it?

BILL. It doesn't seem to be working very well.

GIRL. Yes, well—you did give it quite a bash.

BILL. When?

GIRL. When you fell off your bar stool.

BILL. Was I that drunk?

GIRL. Yes.

BILL. Have you been there all night?

GIRL. I think so.

BILL. *(Closing his eyes.)* What have I done?

GIRL. You really know how to make a girl feel wanted.

BILL. No, you don't understand, I... The point is, today's my... *(Lost for words.)* Oh, my God! Tell me, did we er... ?

GIRL. What?

BILL. Last night... did we... ?

GIRL. You don't remember?

BILL. Well... I'm not sure.

GIRL. *(Quite upset now.)* This gets better and better.

BILL. *(Looks at her.)* But perhaps I do... *(Thinks.)* Yes, I think I do...

GIRL. Make up your mind.

BILL. *(Definite.)* I do. *(In despair.)* Oh my God.

GIRL. You're a real charmer, d'you know that?

BILL. I'm sorry. I'm not very good with alcohol...

GIRL. What are you good with?

BILL. Not a lot really.

(BILL looks under the bedclothes to see if they are wearing anything.)

GIRL. Hey!

BILL. *(Fishing down the bed for his underpants.)* I really am sorry—I don't mean to be insulting...

GIRL. Well you are!

BILL. *(Pulling on his pants under the duvet.)* It's not that... *(Sincere.)* It was wonderful.

GIRL. Thank you.

BILL. But the point is...

GIRL. What?

BILL. I'm getting married.

GIRL. I know.

BILL. Today!

GIRL. I know.

BILL. You know?

GIRL. Yes.

BILL. Well don't you see? This is appalling!

GIRL. I suppose it is, but...

BILL. But what?

GIRL. It happened. I mean, I know it shouldn't have... it's my fault as much as yours... but it happened.

BILL. What am I going to do?

GIRL. Well, I won't tell if you don't.

BILL. Yes, but... *(Has a sudden thought.)* Where are we?

GIRL. The hotel.

BILL. I know, but which room?

GIRL. Um... *(Looks around.)* Looks like the honeymoon suite.

BILL. Oh my God! *(In a panic tries to get out of bed, taking the duvet with him. She squeals and grabs it back. He takes the counterpane instead and wraps it round himself.)* What am I doing here? I shouldn't *be* here! This is booked for tonight. My wedding night. How did I get here?

GIRL. Well, you were *very* drunk.

BILL. I was supposed to have another room, not this one. Not until... *(Shouts.)* Oh, my God!!

GIRL. I do wish you'd stop saying that.

BILL. What's the time?

GIRL *(Peering at her watch.)* Nearly half past nine.

BILL. Rachel! Rachel's coming here!

GIRL. Rachel?

BILL. My fiancee! We booked the suite for today!

GIRL. I thought you booked it for tonight?

BILL. We booked it for today too, so she could change here for the service.

GIRL. Oh my God!

BILL. She'll be here any moment!

GIRL. Why couldn't she dress at home like everyone else?

BILL. It's too far away. There are too many people there. This is disaster! *(Rushes about in the counterpane.)* You must go! You must get out before she gets here! *(She gets out of bed with the duvet wrapped round her. Hurries to collect her scattered clothes.)* Look at the state of this room! *(Picks up the telephone.)* Room service? Can you send someone to do this room, please? As soon as possible! *(Slams the phone down. The door to the reception room next door opens, and TOM appears. He is dressed in a wedding suit, and carries some envelopes and a glass of something fizzy. BILL is helping the GIRL collect her clothes.)* Quickly! Get dressed! She'll be arriving any moment—probably with her bloody mother!

GIRL. All right. Don't panic, don't panic!

TOM. *(Calling.)* Hello!

GIRL. *(Squealing.)* Ahhh!

BILL. Don't panic, don't panic! *(TOM puts the envelopes on a table, and tries the bedroom door handle. It is locked. They freeze. He knocks. BILL is galvanized into action again.)* Quick! *(Tries the door to the passage.)* It's locked! Into the bathroom! Get dressed in there! *(Pushes her towards the bathroom. Stops at the doorway.)* Listen—if you meet anyone, you're the chamber-maid. Do you understand? The chamber-maid! *(She nods. He thrusts her into the bathroom and hurls her remaining clothes after her. Closes the door. Has a thought and opens it again.)* By the way... who are you? *(He has to duck as a toilet brush flies out of the bathroom. Closes the door hurriedly. Another knock from TOM. BILL goes to the other side of the connecting door.)* Who is it?

TOM. Tom.

BILL. Oh, thank God! *(Unlocks the door and opens it.)* Tom—I'm so glad it's you!

TOM. What are you doing here? You're supposed to be in the room across the passage.

BILL. I know. I must have been so drunk last night I got the wrong one. We've booked this one too, you see.

TOM. You don't have to tell me, old son. I did the booking. You look dreadful!

BILL. Yes, well... *(Feeling his head.)* I nearly knocked my head off at some at some stage.

TOM. It was quite an evening. Here's some Alka Seltzer.

BILL. Oh, thank you.

(BILL downs the Alka Seltzer gratefully.)

TOM. I should move if I were you though. Rachel's on her way.

BILL. I know.

TOM. She won't be too pleased to find you sullying her bridal suite prematurely.

BILL. It's worse than you think, Tom.

TOM. What is?

BILL. Tell me—what happened last night?

TOM. What do you mean?

BILL. After our stag night. Where did I go?

TOM. To bed like the rest of us, I presume. You weren't in any condition to do much else.

BILL. Did I ... did I meet anyone?

TOM. Meet anyone?

BILL. I mean... were there any girls around?

TOM. It was a stag night. You don't have girls around on the night before you get married.

BILL. I know, but... Tom, something terrible's happened.

TOM . What? What's the matter?

BILL. I woke up this morning... with a girl beside me.

TOM. Beside you where?

BILL. In bed!

TOM. This bed?

BILL. Yes.

TOM. *(Grinning.)* You jammy bugger!

BILL. No, no—you don't understand.

TOM. I think I do.

BILL. You don't! I don't know who she was!

TOM. You don't know?

BILL. No. I just woke up—with a bump on my head and one hell of a hangover... and there she was.

TOM. In the bed?

BILL. In the bed.

TOM. Wearing what?

BILL. Nothing.

TOM. Well, I've heard of imaginative wedding presents, but that beats them all.

BILL. Where did she come from, Tom?

TOM. Don't ask me, my friend.

BILL. You were here!

TOM. I was as drunk as you were. I staggered off home, and the last I saw you were singing 'You Give Me Fever' to the night porter as he helped you up the stairs.

BILL. I don't understand. How did I find her?

TOM. Room service? *(BILL just looks at him.)* Where is she now?

BILL. Getting dressed in the bathroom.

TOM. Is she pretty?

BILL. Very, but that's not the point!

TOM. It is if you, er... *Did* you, er...

BILL. That's the worst of it. I think we did.

TOM. You think? Don't you remember?

BILL. It's all a bit of a dream.

TOM. God, Bill, you're a case! You have a girl handed to you on a plate and you can't even remember what you did with her!

BILL. Tom, that's not the point. She shouldn't have been here! I'm getting married! To Rachel! *(Points to the window.)* In that church over there, in two hours time!

TOM. I realize that, old son. I am your best man.

BILL. Those fancy-free days are over. I'm going to be a respectable married man.

TOM. Look on it as your last fling.

BILL. It will be if Rachel finds out. *(Paces about.)* God she's right, I'm hopeless. I can't even get my wedding day right. *(Stops.)* How soon will she be here?

TOM. Any moment. *(Takes a mobile phone from his pocket.)* She rang me this morning on my mobile phone...

BILL. Do you two take those damn things everywhere?

TOM. ... to ask if I was awake, which I wasn't, and had I got everything ready, which I hadn't, and did I know how you were, which I didn't...

BILL. Perhaps she'll phone in the wedding ceremony— that would solve all our problems.

TOM. No such luck—I'm under pain of death to see everything's ready for her. Just as well I got here first, eh?

BILL. This is dreadful!

TOM. I knew it was a mistake to have the stag-night and the reception *and* the honeymoon night all in the same place.

BILL. It's the only decent hotel for miles—what else could we do? Look, we must get her out of here. *(Hurries to the bathroom door, and knocks. TOM sees the toilet brush and picks it up.)* Are you nearly ready? *(No response.)* Hello? Are you there?

TOM. What's her name?

BILL. I don't know.

TOM. You didn't even introduce yourselves?

BILL. I can't remember.

TOM. *(Holds up the toilet brush.)* Can you remember what you used this for?

(BILL grabs it from him and turns back to the door.)

BILL. Excuse me, you must leave. My fiancee's going to be here any moment! *(Silence from the bathroom.)* What's she doing?

TOM. Perhaps she's passed out. Was she as drunk as you?

BILL. No. At least she remembered more than I did. *(Knocks on the door again.)* Hello. *(Silence.)* Oh God—this is unbelievable! *(Points at the doors to the landing and to the other room.)* Lock those doors!

TOM. Why?

BILL. In case Rachel turns up!

TOM. *(Locking the connecting door.)* You'd better stop wandering around like Buddha and get dressed.

BILL. *(Hastily pulling on his clothes.)* Where did she come from, Tom, that's what I want to know? Who is she?

TOM. I don't know, but now's not the time to worry about it. *(Trying the door to the landing.)* This door's already locked.

BILL. *(Frantically struggling with his trousers.)* Oh God yes! That means there's only one way out. We must get her out of here! *(Hops to the bathroom door, and hammers on it.)* Please, please! You must come out. She'll be here any second!

(Still no sign from the bathroom.)

TOM. What did you *do* to her?

BILL. She was fine when she got up.

(The door to the reception room opens, and RACHEL appears, carrying a small suitcase and a vanity case.)

RACHEL. Cooee! Tom?

TOM. Rachel!

BILL. Oh God! She's here! What am I going to do?

TOM. Don't panic, don't panic!

(RACHEL puts down the cases and crosses to the connecting door.)

BILL. This is the end! I'll be divorced before I've got married!

(RACHEL tries the door handle. It is locked.)

RACHEL. Tom? Are you in there?

TOM. *(Calling.)* Er ... just a minute.

BILL. *(In a hoarse whisper as he hurriedly completes dressing.)* Tom, there's only one way out of this.

TOM. What?

BILL. You must say she's yours.

TOM. My what?

BILL. Your girlfriend.

TOM. Who is?

BILL. She is! In there!

TOM. She... no!

BILL; Tom!

TOM. No, no, no!

BILL. It's the only way out!

TOM. I've already got a girl-friend. A brand new girlfriend!

BILL. I know, but nobody's met her.

TOM. You're all going to meet her! She's come all the way from London to meet you.

BILL. We haven't met her yet. That could be her!

TOM. It's not her! What do I do with the *real* her?

BILL. Where is the real her?

TOM. At my parents' house—probably half-way through her corn-flakes at this moment.

BILL. That's all right then —she's out of the way.

TOM. She's coming to the wedding! She's looking forward to meeting my best friend, and my best friend's new wife, and all my other friends. What am I supposed to do with her—hide her under my tails?

BILL. This one will have gone by then.,

TOM. It'll be too late by then! Rachel will have met her!

BILL. She won't notice the difference—she'll be too pre-occupied getting married.

TOM. Of course she'll notice! Rachel notices everything! Besides...

BILL. What?

TOM. She knows we were at home. She just telephoned me there.

BILL. On your mobile phone. You could have been anywhere.

RACHEL. *(Knocking.)* Tom?

BILL. *(Frantic.)* Please, Tom!

TOM. I can't! What d'you think she'd say?

BILL. Who?

TOM. Judy.

BILL. Who's Judy?

TOM. *(Apoplectic.)* My girlfriend!

BILL. Why should she say anything?

TOM. Well wouldn't you if you heard I'd spent the night here with another woman?

BILL. She knows you didn't. You spent the night with her, didn't you?

TOM. Of course not—I spent most of it getting drunk with you! If she hears I then spent the rest of it with someone else, it'll be the end—before it's even begun!

RACHEL. *(Through the door.)* Who's that, Tom? Who's in there?

BILL. *(Thrusting the toilet brush into TOM's hands.)* This is an emergency, Tom!

TOM. *(Thrusting the brush back.)* It's your emergency, not mine!

RACHEL. Bill, is that you?

BILL. Oh my God!

RACHEL. *(Hammering on the door.)* Let me in!

BILL. This is it. Good-bye wedding. *(Calls through the door.)* Good morning, darling.

RACHEL. What are you doing in there, Bill? You're supposed to be in the other room.

BILL. It's, er... it's a long story.

RACHEL. Well let me in.

BILL. I don't think that's a good idea.

RACHEL. Why not?

BILL. It's bad luck to meet before the wedding.

RACHEL. Don't be so old-fashioned. Let me in!

BILL. *(Giving him the brush.)* Please, Tom.

TOM. *(Giving it back.)* No!

(BILL takes a deep breath, unlocks the door and goes through, holding the brush, followed by TOM.)

BILL. *(Going to kiss RACHEL.)* Hello, darling.

RACHEL. *(Avoiding the kiss.)* What are you two up to?

BILL. We just, er... we... we...

TOM. Were just going over arrangements.

RACHEL. There are no hitches, are there?

BILL. No, no.

TOM. Not really.

RACHEL. What do you mean, not really?

BILL. Really not. Absolutely not.

RACHEL. I'm looking to you, Tom, to see things go smoothly. I can't trust Bill.

TOM. *(Pointedly.)* No.

BILL. *(Indignant.)* What d'you mean?

RACHEL. Well look at you now—you look awful! What did you get up to last night?

TOM. Good question.

BILL. *(Kicking him.)* We overdid it a bit. *(False enthusiasm.)* But that's all over. Today's the day!

RACHEL. Yes, it is. *(Relents and kisses him.)* And you'd better start getting ready for it, my darling. We've only got a couple of hours, and you can't marry me looking like a brush salesman.

BILL. *(Giving the brush to TOM.)* Are you sure you shouldn't be dressing at home?

RACHEL. It's bedlam at home! All my relatives from around the globe are dressing at home. I want peace and privacy.

BILL. Right.

RACHEL. Now, Mother's coming over with my gown. Father will be here soon too, ordering everyone around as usual. So you go off to your own room, darling, and leave us free to spread around the suite. *(Strokes his cheek provocatively.)* I might let you back in after we're married.

BILL. Er... there is just one thing,, Rachel.

RACHEL. What?

BILL. Can you not use the bedroom just yet.

RACHEL. Why not?

BILL. It, er... well...

TOM. It was used last night.

BILL. They haven't cleaned it up yet.

RACHEL. Who hasn't?

BILL. The chambermaids.

RACHEL. *(Looking at the brush.)* Are you doing it for them?

TOM. Er...

(TOM hands brush back to BILL.)

RACHEL. The suite was supposed to be kept free. They knew we wanted it today.

BILL. I know, but... well, er...

TOM. It got used.

RACHEL. Used?

BILL. Tom used it.

TOM. No, I didn't.

BILL. Yes, he did. I said he could.

RACHEL. Tom?

BILL. He's got his new girlfriend her, you see.

RACHEL. I know. She's coming to the wedding.

BILL. And they couldn't be together at his parents' house.

RACHEL. Be together?

BILL. Sleep together.

RACHEL. Oh. So?

BILL. So I said they could use the suite.

TOM. No, you didn't.

BILL. Yes, I did.

RACHEL. Make up your minds.

BILL. Well, not the suite—just the bedroom.

TOM. But not the bathroom.

BILL. *And* the bathroom.

RACHEL. What are you talking about?

BILL. I said they could sleep here, provided they were out before you got here.

RACHEL. I see.

BILL. But they aren't.

TOM. Yes, they are.

BILL. He is. But she isn't.

RACHEL. What?

BILL. She's in the bathroom.

TOM. No, she isn't.

BILL. Yes, she is.

RACHEL. Do either of you know where she is?

BILL. He's embarrassed. But I said you wouldn't mind. She's getting dressed in the bathroom..

RACHEL. I see.

BILL. So if you could just leave those two rooms free for a while...

RACHEL. How long?

BILL. Not long.

TOM. We hope.

BILL. We hope... you don't mind. I told them you wouldn't mind. You don't mind... do you?

RACHEL. Why should I mind?

BILL. *(To TOM.)* There you are, you see—she doesn't mind.

TOM. Thanks a lot!

RACHEL. What?

TOM. *(To her, with a forced smile.)* Thanks a lot—it's very good of you.

RACHEL. Anything for an old friend.

BILL. So, darling, why don't you and I pop out for a moment.

RACHEL. Why?

BILL. To let them finish.

RACHEL. Finish?

BILL. Getting dressed.

TOM. Good idea.

RACHEL They can finish in there. I'll start in here. Besides I want to meet her.

BILL. You'll meet her at the wedding.

RACHEL. I want to meet her now. Tom's new girlfriend. It's a big moment.

TOM. It probably will be.

RACHEL. What?

BILL. For her too.

TOM. Yes, for her too.

RACHEL. Good.

BILL. Good. Well, um...

RACHEL. You go and get dressed yourself.

BILL. I'll go and get dressed myself.

RACHEL. And take an Alka Seltzer or something.

BILL. I already have.

RACHEL. Then take another one. I don't want you looking like the morning after when it's only the morning before.

BILL. Right.

(Heads for the door to the landing. RACHEL sees the envelopes.)

RACHEL. Oh, are these some good luck messages?

TOM. And your honeymoon plane tickets.

RACHEL. Oh goodie! Give the tickets to Bill to look after.

(RACHEL picks up the messages, and wanders into the bedroom opening them. TOM goes after BILL with the tickets.)

TOM. Bill! *(BILL turns at the door. TOM whispers to him.)* What am I going to do with her?

BILL. *(Whispering back.)* I dunno—keep her as a spare!

TOM. *(Thrusting the tickets at him.)* These are your tickets to Jamaica! Why don't you take her as hand luggage?

BILL. We're overweight already. By the way, I told her to pretend to be the chambermaid.

TOM. The what?

BILL. In case of emergency.

TOM. *Now* you tell me! That would have solved everything.

BILL. No, it wouldn't.

TOM. Why?

BILL. Wait till you see her. No-one would believe it.

TOM. Then why say it?

BILL. It was the best I could think of on the spur of the moment!

(RACHEL returns from the bedroom and closes the door.)

RACHEL. What are you whispering about?

(BILL and TOM turn to her, frozen-faced.)

BILL. Chambermaids.

(BILL hands the brush back to TOM and goes, closing the door in TOM's face. TOM smiles feebly at RACHEL.)

TOM. Yes, chambermaids. I must get one in. And I'll go and hurry whatsername up.

RACHEL. What is her name?

TOM. Who?

RACHEL. Your girlfriend.

TOM. Er... why do you want to know?

RACHEL. It's usual to know people's names when you meet.

TOM. You haven't met yet.

RACHEL. We're just about to. Aren't we?

TOM. Yes...

RACHEL. So what's her name?

TOM. Er... Judy.

RACHEL. Judy.

TOM. Yes.

RACHEL. Right. Introduce me when you're ready.

TOM. Right.

RACHEL. *(Warmly.)* I do hope this one's suitable, Tom. For your sake. *(Turning back to the messages.)* You're our oldest friend.

TOM. *(Muttering.)* I hope it stays that way.

(TOM starts to cross the room towards the bedroom. As he does so, the passage door to the bedroom is unlocked and JULIE enters wearing a chambermaid's overall.)

JULIE. *(Retrieving her key.)* Who locked that, I wonder? *(TOM is hesitating at the connecting door, wondering what to do. Hears the sounds from the bedroom, and listens at the door. JULIE frowns at the unmade bed.)* I thought this room was meant to be empty.

(JULIE crosses towards the bathroom door. TOM turns to see RACHEL staring at him curiously. He smiles feebly and goes through the connecting door, closing it behind him. JULIE turns by the bathroom door, her hand on the knob.)

JULIE. Hello.

TOM. Oh, thank God! You've appeared.

JULIE. What?

TOM. We thought you'd vanished down the plug-hole.

JULIE. Did you want me?

TOM. We've been shouting for you for ages!

JULIE. Oh. I didn't know.

TOM. Are you deaf?

JULIE. Certainly not! Now look here... !

TOM. What were you *doing* in there?

JULIE. In where?

TOM. The bathroom.

JULIE. I was going to clean it up.

TOM. There's no need to do that!

JULIE. *(Looking at the toilet brush.)* Why—are you going to do it for me?

TOM. *(Flinging down the brush.)* And you don't need to dress like that now either.

JULIE. Like what?

TOM. Where did you find that outfit anyway?

JULIE. This outfit?

TOM. Yes.

JULIE. It's the hotel's.

TOM. God—we *could* have got away with it.

JULIE. Got away with what?

TOM. You being the chambermaid. You look the part.

JULIE. Thanks very much!

TOM. Well it's too late now.

JULIE. Look, what are you talking about? Who are you?

TOM. Oh, sorry. I'm Tom.

JULIE. Tom?

TOM. Bill's best friend. *(She looks blank.)* The best man.

JULIE. Best man?

TOM. Yes.

JULIE. Oh, for the wedding!

TOM. Of course for the wedding! The divorce comes later.

JULIE. Yes, I know about the wedding.

TOM. Well I wish you'd thought about it earlier.

JULIE. I beg your pardon?

TOM. You aren't exactly helping much, are you?

JULIE. *(Indignant.)* I'm doing my best!

TOM. It's a bit late now. You'd have done better to have thought about it last night.

JULIE. I wasn't on duty last night.

TOM. It sounds as if you were very much on duty last night.

JULIE. Are you being rude?

TOM. I've every right to be! I'm in a hell of a spot now.

JULIE. Are you?

TOM. And so is Bill!

JULIE. Why?

TOM. His fiancee's in the next room. And that's the only way out!

JULIE. And where's he?

TOM. Done a bunk. Leaving me to hold the baby.

JULIE. They've got a baby?

TOM. Are you trying to be funny?

JULIE. I'm sorry. I've lost the thread of this conversation.

TOM. Look, what's happened has happened. There's no point in me going over it all with you now...

JULIE. I'm glad of that. But what... ?

TOM. And there's no time to ask questions. You've got to help me save Bill's skin.

JULIE. Me?

TOM. Yes.

JULIE. Why?

TOM. You don't want his big day ruined, do you?

JULIE. Of course not.

TOM. O.K. he went overboard last night—it could happen to anyone...

JULIE. *(A glimmer dawning.)* Ohhh, I see...

TOM. But now we've got to get him back on the rails.

JULIE. How can I help?

TOM. A little play acting—that's all that's needed.

JULIE. Play acting?
TOM. Yes.
JULIE. *(Dubiously.)* Well I think I can handle that.
TOM. Good.
JULIE. I played Ophelia for the local amateurs.
TOM. How did the mad scene go?
JULIE. What?
TOM. Never mind. This role won't be so difficult.
JULIE. What is it?
TOM. My girlfriend.

(Pause.)

JULIE. Your what?
TOM. You see, Rachel's found out this room was used last night.
JULIE. *(Looking at the ravaged bed.)* It certainly was!
TOM. Yes, well we needn't go into that, thank you. The point is we had to think very fast. We told her it was I and my girlfriend who were in here.
JULIE. You and your girlfriend?
TOM. That's you and me.
JULIE. Me and you?
TOM. Yes.
JULIE. In here?
TOM. Yes.
JULIE. Doing what?
TOM. *(Furious.)* What do you think?
JULIE. *(Bewildered.)* But why me?
TOM. You're the one who's in here! Who else could it have been?
JULIE. *(Looking around helplessly.)* Well, I er...
TOM. *(Patiently.)* Look, listen carefully, please. It obviously doesn't concern you over-much, but it's important you understand the situation here.
JULIE. I'd love to understand it.

TOM. Very well. Rachel and Bill are getting married today, right?

JULIE. Right.

TOM. For whatever reason, Bill spent the night in here with another woman, right?

JULIE. *(Wide-eyed.)* Ah—I see!

TOM. And if Rachel found out all hell would break loose, and the marriage would go down the tubes, right?

JULIE. Right!

TOM. Thank God for that! So Bill's only hope is to convince her it wasn't him in here, but someone else. And the only someone else who happens to be around is this poor sucker here—me. So if we can persuade Rachel that you are my girlfriend, and you and I spent the night in here together, then with any luck we can get out with Bill's reputation still intact, and then you can go your own merry way and forget the whole thing ever happened—right?

JULIE. Right... I think.

TOM. *(With a sigh.)* At last!

JULIE. Though I don't see why we should help him.

TOM. You don't?

JULIE. If he's unfaithful the night before his wedding day, he deserves all he gets.

TOM. That's rich!

JULIE. What?

TOM. Who are you to criticize him?

JULIE. I've every right to criticize him! Just because I don't know him doesn't mean I can't have an opinion about such matters.

TOM. Don't you think it might have been a good idea to *get* to know him a bit!

JULIE. I've got a job to do! I can't get to know every customer, can I?

(A beat.)

TOM. Customer? *(Revelation.)* Oh, I see! He's a customer.

JULIE. Well of course he's a customer!

TOM. So *that's* where you came from!

JULIE. Eh?

TOM. You're sort of ... regularly on call here.

JULIE. Naturally.

TOM. *(Looking round with new eyes.)* Good Lord! I didn't realize it was that sort of place.

JULIE. *(Flummoxed.)* You what?

TOM. Well, it just looks like a nice country house hotel, doesn't it? But I suppose these days you have to provide all amenities.

JULIE. Of course you do.

TOM. *(Chuckling.)* I bet it was that night porter who suggested it.

JULIE. George?

TOM. Is it him who calls you?

JULIE. When I'm wanted, yes.

TOM. *(Nodding.)* And Bill was so pissed he fell for it.

JULIE. Fell for what?

TOM. Getting in a call-girl.

JULIE. Getting in a ... ?

TOM. Yes.

JULIE. *(Light dawning.)* Oh, is that what happened?

TOM. You tell me.

JULIE. George fixed it up for a lark, and your friend was so drunk after his stag party that he didn't know what he was doing.

TOM. Exactly.

JULIE. Ah.

TOM. Did he?

JULIE. What?

TOM. Know what he was doing.

JULIE. When?

TOM. When he, er ... got into bed.

JULIE. *(Looking at the bed.)* Not much doubt about that! Look at the state of the bed.

TOM. Well, you should know.

JULIE. *(Indignant.)* Not all customers behave like him, you know.

TOM. Wow! Dear old Bill. He's certainly going out in style!

JULIE. Here! Where's the duvet gone?

TOM. Never mind about that now. You and I have to perform our act. Now get those things off.

JULIE. I *beg* your pardon!

TOM. The maid's things.

JULIE. Oh. *(Taking off her chambermaid's overall.)* Right.

TOM. And by the way, your name's Judy.

JULIE. It's not—it's Julie.

TOM. *(Long suffering.)* Your name as my girlfriend.

JULIE. Oh, right.

TOM. God, you're making this heavy-going!

(A nervous BILL re-enters next door.)

BILL. Hello.

RACHEL. Haven't you changed yet?

BILL. There's no hurry, sweetheart. Has, er ... Tom's girlfriend appeared yet?

RACHEL. Not yet. What do you want?

BILL. I just wanted to be here when you met her.

RACHEL. Why?

BILL. Oh, just to, er ... make sure all goes smoothly...

RACHEL. She's just a girlfriend, darling—not the Tax Inspector.

BILL. No, but—welL..

(TOM sticks his head through the connecting door.)

TOM. Ah. You're still there.

RACHEL. Of course I'm still here.

TOM. Just checking. Thought you might have wanted to pop down and see if your mother's arrived, or something.

RACHEL. She can find her own way.

TOM. Yes.

(A beat.)

RACHEL. Well, where is she?

TOM. Your mother?

RACHEL. No, you fool—your girlfriend!

TOM. Ah, yes, er ... right here.

RACHEL. Then let me meet her.

(TOM reluctantly ushers JULIE through.)

TOM. Here we are then. Judy—this is Rachel, Bill's fiancee.

JULIE. Hello.

TOM. And Rachel, this is Judy, my girlfriend.

RACHEL. Hello.

BILL. *(Aghast.)* No, it isn't.

RACHEL. *(About to shake hands with JULIE.)* What?

JULIE. What?

BILL. That's not her!

TOM. Eh?

JULIE. Eh?

RACHEL. What do you mean?

BILL. *(Floundering.)* That's not... I mean that's not the girlfriend I though it was.

TOM. Yes, it is.

BILL. No, it isn't.

RACHEL. What are you talking about?

BILL. I mean that ... I thought Tom's girlfriend ... was a different girl ... who wasn't the same girl ... as this one...

TOM. Different?

BILL. Yes.

RACHEL. Are you being a bit tactless, darling?

BILL. Tactless?

RACHEL. I don't know how many girlfriends Tom has, but now is not really the time to bring it up.

BILL. Er... no, of course not. *(Shakes hand with JULIE.)* How d'you do?

RACHEL. Haven't you met?

BILL. No ... Yes ... Er, only sort of.

RACHEL. Sort of?

TOM. *(Coming to the rescue.)* She wasn't properly dressed at the time.

RACHEL. Oh, I see. *(Brightly.)* Well, it's nice to meet you, Judy. You must excuse my extremely undiplomatic fiance. I'm sure the other girlfriends are nothing to worry about.

JULIE. That's all right. I don't mind how many he has.

RACHEL. How very broad-minded.

JULIE. Oh I am.

(BILL is gesticulating at TOM behind RACHEL's back.)

RACHEL. Well, Bill?

(RACHEL turns and sees BILL. He hurriedly turns his movements into physical jerks.)

BILL. Working off my hang-over.

RACHEL. You're behaving very oddly this morning. Is it the wedding? Are you in shock or something.

BILL. A bit.

TOM. Me too.

RACHEL. Well you'd both better pull yourselves together. The service is less than two hours time, and I don't want you behaving like freaks throughout.

BILL. No. Well I just want a word in private with these two, darling...

(BILL waves TOM and JULIE through to the bedroom.)

RACHEL. What for?

BILL. Just to makes sure all the arrangements are ready. *(Almost hurls TOM through the door.)* I don't want you to have to worry about anything.

(BILL pulls JULIE through with him, and closes the connecting door. RACHEL stares at the door for a moment, then goes to her vanity case, and starts to put her hair up.)

BILL. *(To TOM.)* Right—who the hell is this?

TOM. Who?

BILL. *(Pointing at JULIE.)* This!

TOM. Isn't it who you said it was?

JULIE. Who *did* he say it was?

BILL. None of your business!

JULIE. I beg your pardon! It certainly is my business!

BILL. *(To TOM, pointing at the bathroom.)* I said you were to say that one was your girlfriend, not go out and find another one!

JULIE. Another what?

TOM. She is that one.

BILL. No, she isn't.

JULIE. That one what?

TOM. Well, that's where she came from.

BILL. She can't have done.

TOM. I saw her!

JULIE. Saw me what?

TOM. *(To her.)* Didn't I see you coming out of the bathroom?

JULIE. No, you saw me going into the bathroom.

BILL. You can't have been—someone else was in the bathroom.

TOM. Who else was in the bathroom?

BILL. That's what you were supposed to find out.

TOM. Well, there's no-one in the bathroom now.

BILL. How do you know if you didn't see anybody coming out?

TOM. *(Going to the bathroom door.)* I told you, I saw *her* coming out.

JULIE. No, you didn't.

TOM. Yes, I did. And what is more... *(Tries the door. It is still locked.)* There's someone in the bathroom.

JULIE. There you are.

BILL. You see?

TOM. *(To JULIE.)* Who is it?

JULIE. Don't ask me.

TOM. Well, if you didn't come out of there...

JULIE. Yes?

TOM. Who are you?

JULIE. The chambermaid.

TOM. No. Forget that story. Who *are* you?

JULIE. The chambermaid.

BILL. The chambermaid?

TOM. She can't be.

BILL. Why not?

TOM. She's a call girl.

(JULIE slaps TOM's face.)

JULIE. I certainly am not a call girl!

TOM. You said you were a call girl!

(JULIE slaps TOM again.)

JULIE. I did *not* say I was a call girl! *(Points at the bathroom.)* You said she was a call girl.

TOM. *(Dazed.)* I'm going out of my mind.

BILL. Look, let's start again from the beginning. Where did you come from?

JULIE. Downstairs.

BILL. How did you get in here?

JULIE. Through that door.

TOM. She can't have done.

JULIE. Why not?

BILL. It's locked.

JULIE. I unlocked it.

TOM. *(Going to the door.)* She can't have done!

JULIE. I did.

TOM. *(Opening the door.)* She did.

BILL. How did you unlock it?

JULIE. I'm the chambermaid.

TOM. *(Returning.)* She *can't* be the chamber maid!

BILL. *(To JULIE.)* Did you *say* you were the chamber maid?

JULIE. Of course I said I was the chambermaid!

BILL. *(To TOM.)* Did you hear her say she was the chambermaid?

TOM. You *told* me she'd say she was the chambermaid!

BILL. *(To JULIE.)* How do we know you're the chambermaid?

JULIE. *(Picking up her chambermaid's overall.)* Why d'you think I was wearing this if I wasn't the chambermaid?

BILL. You were wearing that?

JULIE. Yes.

BILL. *(To TOM.)* She was wearing that?

TOM. *(Dumbly.)* Yes.

(Pause.)

TOM & BILL. *(Together.)* She's the chambermaid!

JULIE. Well, I'm glad we've got that sorted out. *(Puts down the overall. To BILL.)* You should know—it was presumably you who sent for me.

TOM. You sent for her?

BILL. So I did. I'd forgotten.

TOM. Christ almighty! You mean we went through all that for nothing?

BILL. I'm very sorry. *(Pointing at the bathroom.)* But if she's the chambermaid, who the hell is that?

TOM. *I* don't know!

JULIE. It's a call girl.

BILL. A call girl?

JULIE. Yes.

BILL. How do you know?

JULIE. He said so.

TOM. No, I didn't.

JULIE. Yes, you did.

BILL. How did *you* know?

TOM. I didn't. I've never met her.

JULIE. You told me you had met her.

TOM. No, I didn't!

JULIE. Yes, you did!

BILL. Silence!! *(They silence. He takes a deep breath and speaks slowly and carefully.)* Let's forget for the moment who's met who, and who is what, and who said what to who.

TOM. Right.

JULIE. Right.

BILL. The point is, where did she come from?

TOM. George got her.

BILL. George?

TOM. Yes.

BILL. Who's George?

JULIE. The night porter.

BILL. The night porter.

JULIE. Yes.

BILL. Why did he get her?

TOM. Presumably because you ordered her.

BILL. *(Stunned.)* I ordered her!

JULIE. Well it's unlikely anyone else ordered her.

BILL. Bloody hell! I must have been drunk out of my mind!

TOM. *(Singing.)* You give me fever...

BILL. Shut up! *(TOM shuts up.)* This gets worse and worse! *(Decisively.)* Right, this is what we do. Tom—you go next door and keep Rachel out of the way for a few more moments. *(To JULIE.)* You—what's your name?

JULIE. Julie.

BILL. Julie—you go and get whatever it is you need to make the bed and put this room straight.

JULIE. Right.

BILL. And I'll get whoever it is in there, out of there, and then out of here, and then—with any luck—we can all start again at the beginning.

TOM. How are you going to get her out of there? You couldn't get her out before.

· BILL. I'm a desperate man now. I'll break down the door if I have to. Right—move. *(They all move in different directions.)* Tom! *(They stop.)* Just don't pick up anyone else on your way.

TOM. It's not very likely.

BILL. Julie. *(They stop again.)* Tell George—no more call girls, whoever orders them.

JULIE. No more call girls.

(She goes out of the passage door. TOM goes through the connecting door. BILL goes to listen at the bathroom door.)

TOM. *(To RACHEL.)* Well, that's sorted that out.

RACHEL. What?

TOM. Julie.

RACHEL. Julie?

TOM. Judy.

RACHEL. Make up your mind. *(He grins foolishly.)* How many girl friends *have* you got, Tom?

TOM. Oh, just one or two.

RACHEL. Never could make up your mind. We all thought it was going to be *the* one this time.

TOM. Oh it is the one... It's just that last time, the other one ... seemed to be the one ... but turned out to be ... just another one ... so I sometimes mix her up with this one ... who really is the one.

RACHEL. Ah. Where's Bill?

TOM. With the other one.

RACHEL. What?

TOM. Er ... in the other room. Giving the chambermaid instructions.

RACHEL. *(Happily.)* For tonight?

TOM. Yes, that's right. He wants to make sure that you get everything you expect ... I mean, that you...

RACHEL. I know what you mean, Tom.

(He collapses on the sofa, worn out. RACHEL gets on with her toilette. Next door, BILL knocks on the bathroom door.)

BILL. Excuse me. *(Tries the door. It is still locked.)* Excuse me, you must come out now. This can't go on any longer. If you don't come out I'm going to have to force the door. *(Pause. The sound of a lock turning. The door opens. The girl comes out. They gaze at each other.)* Hello.

GIRL. Hello.

BILL. At last.

GIRL. Sorry.

BILL. What were you *doing* in there?

GIRL. Hiding.

BILL. From my fiancee?

GIRL. No.

BILL. From the chambermaid?

GIRL. No.

BILL. Then who?

GIRL. Tom.

BILL. *(Puzzled.)* From Tom?

GIRL. Yes.

BILL. Why?

GIRL. I'm his girlfriend.

(Pause.)

BILL. His girlfriend's at home.

GIRL. No.

BILL. With his parents.

GIRL., No.
BILL. Having corn flakes.
GIRL. No.
BILL. *(Stunned.)* You're Judy?
GIRL. Yes.
BILL. Oh my God! *(Pause.)* How did it happen?
JUDY. Don't you remember?
BILL. Not a lot.
JUDY. Oh.
BILL. At least...
JUDY. Yes?
BILL. I thought it was a dream.
JULY. It was. Sort of.
BILL. A lovely dream.
JUDY. I'm glad you said that.
BILL. What?
JUDY. Lovely.
BILL. But we can't.
JULY. No.
BILL. We shouldn't have.
JULY. No.
BILL. We mustn't.
JUDY. Definitely not.

(There is a vibrant moment. They turn away from each other.)

BILL. Oh God! *(Pause.)* What do we do now?
JUDY. Where's Tom?
BILL. Next door.
JUDY. With Rachel?
BILL. Yes.
JUDY. Oh.
BILL. How did you know he was here?
JUDY. I could hear his voice through the door.
BILL. Did you hear him with the chambermaid?
JUDY. Yes. Fool!

BILL. Just as well, in the circumstances.

JUDY. Yes.

BILL. So did George get you here?

JUDY. I beg your pardon?

BILL. The night porter.

JUDY. What d'you mean?

BILL. Well, did he call you?

JUDY. Call me?

BILL. *(Patiently.)* When I called for a call girl, was it you he called?

JUDY. *Call* girl?

BILL. Isn't that what you are? *(JUDY slaps his face. He recovers.)* Sorry.

JUDY. I should think so!

BILL. Tom told me you were.

JUDY. He *what*?

BILL. *(Befuddled.)* No, that can't be right.

JUDY. Would Tom take a call girl for a girlfriend?

BILL. No.

JUDY. Well, then.

BILL. I'm glad of that!

JUDY. You have a genius for making a girl feel good, d'you know that?

BILL. I'm very sorry—I really am. It's just ... I'm still in a bit of a daze about what happened.

JUDY. Well I'll leave you to think about it. I'd better get out of here before someone comes in.

BILL. You can't go now.

JUDY. I can't stay here.

BILL. But you can't just... I mean, we can't just...

JUDY. Yes, we can. We have to. *(Goes to the door.)* I'll see you at the wedding.

BILL. I wish I could remember.

JUDY. Perhaps it's best that you don't.

(JUDY turns to the door. At that moment it opens and JULIE

enters carrying clean linen for the bed.)

JULIE. Oh, you've come out.

JUDY. Yes.

JULIE. That's good. You shouldn't have been here in the first place, you know.

JUDY. I know.

JULIE. We're not that sort of a hotel.

JUDY. I beg your pardon?

BILL. Er, Julie...

JULIE. Come to that, you don't look that sort of girl.

JUDY. Now look here!

BILL. Julie...

JULIE. *(To BILL.)* And as for you, you should be ashamed of yourself!

BILL. Julie, it's not...

JULIE. *(Putting the linen on the bed.)* The night before your wedding! Really!

BILL. I know, but you see...

JULIE. Don't try and excuse yourself to me. I don't know how I got into this. If the manager found out I was involved in a call girl racket I'd be in the soup!

JUDY. This has gone too far!

BILL. Julie, will you listen to me... !

(They are interrupted by a telephone ringing. Everyone turns to look at the room phones.)

JULIE. *(To BILL.)* Well, it's your suite. Answer it.

BILL. Er...

(BILL apprehensively picks up the phone. Next door RACHEL answers the phone there.)

RACHEL. Hello?

BILL. Hello?

RACHEL. *(Frowning.)* Bill?
BILL. Rachel?
RACHEL. What's going on?

(The phone ring sounds again.)

TOM. *(Taking out his mobile phone.)* Oh, it's my phone.
RACHEL. *(Impatient.)* Oh for heaven's sake!

(RACHEL and BILL replace their phones.)

TOM. *(Answering his phone.)* Hello?

(RACHEL goes towards the connecting door.)

RACHEL. *(Crossly.)* What are they doing in there? I need
the bedroom.
TOM. *(On the phone.)* Yes. Oh, Really?

*(RACHEL opens the connecting door and goes through. She
stops on seeing the other three.)*

BILL. Ah.
RACHEL. What's happening here?
BILL. We were just going, darling.
RACHEL. *(Looking at JUDY.)* Who's this?
JUDY. Er...
BILL. The chambermaid.
JULIE. Now, look...
JUDY. *(Quickly.)* Yes, the chambermaid. *(Picks up JULIE's
overall.)* I've come to change the bed.

*(JUDY puts on the overall, picks up the linen and starts to
make the bed.)*

JULIE. Thank you very much!

RACHEL. What?

JULIE. *(With a sweet smile.)* I'm just saying thank you very much.

RACHEL. Well, do you think I could take possession of the suite now? I do have to get ready for a wedding, you know.

BILL. Yes, darling, of course. We, er ... we were just helping the, er ... chambermaid to clear up, and then it's all yours.

JULIE. *(To RACHEL.)* You're quite sure about this wedding, are you?

RACHEL. I beg your pardon?

JULIE. I mean, you're quite positive he's the right man for you?

RACHEL. Of course I am!

JULIE. Just wondered.

RACHEL. Why shouldn't I be?

JULIE. Well, it's a big decision for a girl. You should be certain you know the man you're going to marry.

RACHEL. I've known him all my life!

JULIE. *(With a pointed look at BILL.)* Ah, but does that mean you can trust him?

RACHEL. Of course I can trust him! *(To BILL.)* Can't I?

BILL. Of course she can trust me.

JULIE. Well, just as long as you're sure. It is for the *rest* of your life, after all.

RACHEL. What are you talking about? You've only just met us. I really don't think it's your place to start lecturing us on our wedding morning.

JULIE. If you say so.

RACHEL. *(Indicating JUDY.)* And in front of the hotel staff too.

JUDY. *(Quickly.)* Er, the duvet. Where's the duvet?

BILL. Isn't it in the bathroom?

JUDY. Oh, yes. Silly me.

(JUDY goes to get it. Next door TOM switches off his mobile phone.)

RACHEL. What's the duvet doing in the bathroom?
JULIE. Good question.
BILL. Haven't the faintest idea.

(TOM comes through, frowning.)

TOM. That was my mother.
RACHEL. What did she want?
TOM. Judy's not at home.

(The door to the bathroom slams shut. They all turn and stare at it.)

RACHEL. *(Turning back.)* Not at home?
TOM. No.
RACHEL. Of course not. *(Indicating JULIE.)* She's here.
TOM. *(Caught.)* Ah— ha, ha, of course she is.
RACHEL. You knew she was.
TOM. Yes, but ... my mother didn't.
RACHEL. Didn't she?
TOM. She thought she was at home ... but when she realized she wasn't ... she wondered where she was.
RACHEL. So what did you tell her?
TOM. She was here.
RACHEL. Then that's all right then.
TOM. Yes.
RACHEL. But since everybody seems to be here, can I ask you to all go elsewhere, because I'm the only one who's *meant* to be here.
BILL. Right.
TOM. Right.

(RACHEL looks at JULIE.)

JULIE. Right.

(They all move towards the connecting door.)

RACHEL. And the chambermaid too.
JULIE. I'm just going.
BILL. *(Hissing.)* Not you!
JULIE. *(Quickly.)* Not me. The chambermaid.
RACHEL. That's what I said. Can you ask her for me, darling?
BILL. Right ... yes ... I'll ask her. *(To JULIE and TOM.)* You carry on.
RACHEL. Oh, bring my cases through for me, would you please, Tom.

(BILL freezes on his way to the bathroom.)

TOM. Right.
RACHEL. *(Seeing BILL.)* Go on, Bill.
BILL. Right. *(TOM and JULIE go through the connecting door. BILL goes to the bathroom and opens the door.)* Would you mind finishing in here now, please.

(BILL frantically gestures into the bathroom for JUDY to stay there. TOM returns with the suitcase and vanity case.)

RACHEL. Thank you , Tom. You can put the vanity case in the bathroom.
BILL. Er, why the bathroom, darling?
RACHEL. I want to have a bath. Why not the bathroom?
BILL. Oh ... just thought you might want to do it somewhere else.
RACHEL. What *is* the matter with you this morning?

(TOM has put down the suitcase and is heading towards the bathroom with the vanity case. BILL is transfixed in the bathroom doorway. At that moment JUDY pushes past him with the duvet held up in front of her.)

JUDY. *(With a cockney accent.)* Found the duvet, sir.

(JUDY passes TOM, hidden behind the duvet. He gives her a curious glance and continues into the bathroom.)

BILL. Just leave it on the bed. We'll see to it.
JUDY. Right, sir.
RACHEL. Oh, she can make up the bed now she's here. I'll be in the bathroom.
BILL. Right.
JUDY. Right.

(JUDY starts to put the clean duvet cover on. BILL hovers.)

RACHEL. Run along, darling.
BILL. Right.

(BILL goes through the connecting door. TOM comes out of the bathroom and crosses towards the other room. JUDY dives into the bed, buried in the duvet cover.)

TOM. *(To RACHEL.)* I'll leave you to it then.
RACHEL. Thank you, Tom. By the way, have you put up the table plans yet?
TOM. No, I was just going to, er...
RACHEL. And have you got the place cards?
TOM. Yes, I was just going to, er...
RACHEL. Time's getting on, Tom.
TOM. Yes.

(TOM glances at JUDY's behind, bend over the bed, and goes through the connecting door. Closes it.)

TOM. *(To BILL.)* What happened?
BILL. Who to?
TOM. The girl!

BILL. She, er ... she's gone.

TOM. Then who's that?

BILL. Who?

TOM. In there?

BILL. Rachel.

TOM. No, you fool! The other one.

BILL. The chambermaid.

JULIE. Eh?

TOM. *(Indicating JULIE.)* She's the chambermaid.

JULIE. Quite.

BILL. That's another one.

JULIE. Eh?

BILL. *(Waving at her.)* Shh.

TOM. Where did she come from?

BILL. I sent for her.

TOM. What for?

BILL. To do the bed.

JULIE. Eh?

BILL. Shh!

TOM. It's odd.

BILL. What?

TOM. I seemed to ... recognize her.

BILL. Seemed to?

TOM. Well I only saw her rear end.

BILL. Are you an authority on chambermaids' rear ends?

JULIE. Not on mine, he isn't.

TOM. Never mind. *(Takes BILL to one side.)* Bill, I'm worried.

BILL. What about?

TOM. Judy isn't at home.

BILL. Isn't she?

TOM. She hasn't been at home all night.

BILL. How do you know?

TOM. Mother says her bed hasn't been slept in.

BILL. Perhaps she slept on the floor.

TOM. Don't be stupid. *(JULIE has sidled up to listen. He notices her.)* Do you mind?

JULIE. Not at all.

TOM. *(Taking BILL aside again.)* You see ... I didn't tell you, but I had a row with her last night.

BILL. With your mother?

TOM. With Judy!

BILL. Oh. What about?

TOM. About her being left on her own. It was the first time we'd been away together, you see, and when she found out she wasn't invited to the stag party she got rather upset.

(JULIE is sidling up to hear again.)

BILL. Surely she knew that girls don't go to stag parties?

TOM. Yes, but ... Well, you see, we'd rather planned this weekend as our first...

BILL. First what?

TOM. Well, I'd made up my mind this was *the* one at last... and I'd finally got her to agree to...

BILL. To what?

TOM. Well, it was going to be the big moment.

BILL. What big moment?

JULIE. Use your imagination!

TOM. Excuse me, but this doesn't really concern you!

JULIE. On the contrary, it concerns me quite a lot.

TOM. How do you work that out?

JULIE. If I'm supposed to be replacing someone to whom a big moment is going to be happening, then I'd rather like to know what the big moment's going to be!

TOM. Well you needn't worry—it isn't likely to happen to you.

JULIE. Thank you, I'm glad of that!

TOM. *(Taking BILL aside again.)* So you see, she was rather put out when she found I was going to be out ... leaving her in

... until I came back in ... and then expected her to put out... so to speak.

JULIE. *(Who has followed.)* I should think she was!

TOM. I'm talking to Bill!

BILL. What did she say when you came back in?

TOM. That's just it—I didn't see her when I came back in. Her door was closed, and I was drunk, and we'd had a hell of a row ... and quite frankly I didn't dare try to disturb her.

BILL. Ah.

TOM. Then this morning her door was still closed, so I thought it best to let sleeping dogs lie, and came on over here without seeing her. And now my mother says she wasn't there anyway. *(Confidentially.)* Do you know what I think?

BILL. What?

JULIE. What?

TOM. I think she's gone back to London in a huff.

JULIE. What's wrong with the trains?

(JULIE giggles at her own wit.)

TOM. Look, this isn't funny!

JULIE. Sorry.

TOM. *(To BILL.)* What do you think?

BILL. No, it isn't funny.

TOM. Not that! About her going to London?

BILL. She wouldn't do that.

TOM. No, she's not that kind of a girl.

JULIE. Perhaps she's gone off with somebody else.

BILL. No, she's not that kind of a girl.

TOM. How do you know?

BILL. Well ... you're not the kind of man who'd go out with that kind of girl.

TOM. No.

BILL. The kind of girl you'd go with wouldn't go with somebody else just when you were going to have your big moment.

JULIE. You did.

BILL. Do you mind keeping out of this!

JULIE. Well I think you're both as bad as each other. You don't deserve any big moments, either of you.

TOM. Listen, Oprah, haven't you got some beds to make or something?

JULIE. Oh, I see. You've finished with my services, have you?

TOM. Yes, thank you.

JULIE. Having helped you out of the scrape you'd got yourselves into, you now feel you don't need me any longer.

BILL. Helped us out? You made it worse!

JULIE. I did everything I was asked to do. It's you two who don't know your call girls from your chambermaids. *(To BILL, pointing next door.)* Talking of which, what was all that about her being a chambermaid?

BILL. *(Glancing at TOM.)* Look, just be quiet and don't ask any questions for once in your life!

JULIE. Huh! Well, I've got work to do if I want to keep my job.

TOM. So've I! I've still got to put out the table plans and the place cards. *(Looks at his watch. To BILL.)* And so've you, if you're going to be at the altar on time.

BILL. Oh God—I never wanted this sort of over-the-top wedding in the first place!

(They all try to get out of the passage door together. They all step back.)

TOM. One at a time.

(Next door, JUDY has finished making up the bed.)

JUDY. *(To RACHEL.)* I'll leave you now, madam.

RACHEL. Right, thank you.

(JUDY goes out of the bedroom door just as TOM goes out of the other door.)

JULIE. *(To BILL.)* After you—sir.
BILL. No, after you.

(Before they can move, TOM and JUDY return and slam their respective doors.)

RACHEL. What is it?
BILL. *(Next door.)* What is it?
JUDY. Er ... I forgot the dirty linen.

(JUDY goes to collect it.)

TOM. I saw her!
BILL. Who?
TOM. Judy.
BILL. Where?
TOM. Out there. *(Indicates the bedroom.)* Coming out of there.
BILL. No, no— can't have been.
TOM. It was, I tell you!
BILL. It can't have been!
TOM. *(Going to the connecting door.)* It was! *(On the other side, Judy is hesitating between the two doors. She, too, chooses the connecting door. She opens it, and they come face to face.)* Judy!
JUDY. Tom!
BILL. Oh Lord!
TOM. What are you doing here?
JUDY. Er ...
TOM. Well?
JUDY. Looking for you.
TOM. Where've you been?
JUDY. Er...

RACHEL. *(Curiously.)* What's going on? Who is this?

JUDY. Er...

TOM. This, Rachel, is ... *(Stops.)* Ah.

RACHEL. Who?

TOM. Er...

RACHEL. You called her Judy.

TOM. Did I?

RACHEL. I thought the other one was Judy.

TOM. Julie. This one's Julie.

RACHEL. The chambermaid.

JUDY. Yes.

TOM. Yes.

RACHEL. Why was she looking for you?

TOM. Was she?

RACHEL. She just said so.

JUDY. Because I heard he was looking for me.

RACHEL. Why was he looking for you?

TOM. To, er... come and do the bed.

JUDY. Yes.

RACHEL. You saw her doing the bed.

TOM. I mean, I was looking for her before I saw her. But now I've seen her, I don't need to look for her.

RACHEL. How do you know her?

TOM. I don't.

RACHEL. You called her Judy.

TOM. Julie.

RACHEL. Whatever. And she called you Tom.

TOM. They told me she was Julie when I was looking for her.

JUDY. And they told me it was Tom who was looking for me.

.RACHEL. *(Puzzled.)* Oh, I see.

TOM. Anyway, Julie, have you finished in there now?

JUDY. Yes.

TOM. Well, come in here, and leave Rachel to get ready for her wedding.

JUDY. Right.
TOM. *(To RACHEL.)* Right?
RACHEL. *(Bemused.)* Right.

(JUDY and TOM go through to the other room, where the other two are still waiting, transfixed. TOM closes the connecting door, and collapses against it with a sigh of relief.)

TOM. Whew! That was a close one.
BILL. It certainly was.
TOM. *(To JUDY.)* You were very quick there, Judy.
JUDY. Thank you.
TOM. If Rachel had found out what you were doing here... Just a minute. What *are* you doing here?
JUDY. Er...
BILL. *(Quickly.)* She's pretending to be the chambermaid.
JUDY. Yes.
TOM. Why?
BILL. *(Indicating JULIE.)* Because this chambermaid wasn't available.
JULIE. No.
TOM. How did she know?
BILL. Know what?
TOM. About all that!
BILL. I told her.
TOM. When?
BILL. When I was getting rid of the other one.
TOM. Which other one?
BILL. You know. The other girl.
TOM. Oh, the call girl!
JUDY. The what?
BILL. Yes—that one. I took her downstairs, while you were in here. And in the foyer I bumped into Judy.
TOM. What was she doing in the foyer?
JUDY. Looking for you.
BILL. Yes, looking for you. So when I realized who it was,

I thought that, since Julie was pretending to be her, she could pretend to be Julie.

TOM. Why?

BILL. In case Rachel asked for another chambermaid, and the hotel wondered what had happened to Julie.

TOM. Why didn't you tell me?

BILL. What?

TOM. That you'd found Judy.

BILL. I just did.

TOM. Before. When I told you I'd lost her.

BILL. Didn't I?

TOM. When I told you I recognized her rear end.

JUDY. What?

TOM. Er—sorry. It's a very nice rear end.

BILL. Yes, it is.

TOM. (Sharply.) What?

BILL. Nothing.

TOM. Why didn't you tell me then?

BILL. (Stumped.) I er...

TOM. (Aggressive.) Well?

BILL. Um ... your tie's a bit crooked, you know...

(BILL tries to straighten it.)

TOM. (Brushing him away.) Now, look... !

JUDY. (Quickly.) He was trying to protect me.

BILL. That's right.

TOM. From what?

BILL. Er... (To JUDY.) From what?

JUDY. You see, Tom, I ... I spent the night here last night.

TOM. What?

BILL. (Aghast.) Judy ...

JUDY. I was so upset after our row that I came here to look for you, and when I couldn't find you, I couldn't face going back to your parents' house, so I stayed here at the hotel

TOM. Where? All the rooms were booked for wedding guests.

JUDY. *(Pointing.)* Over there.

TOM. Over there?

JUDY. The room Bill was meant to have.

TOM. Bill's room?

JUDY. I met him on the landing. He was so drunk he didn't know where he was, so I helped him. I found he had two keys in his pocket, so I put him in this room and I took that room.

BILL. *(Relieved.)* That's right.

TOM. How do you know?

BILL. Know what?

TOM. You were too drunk to know where you were.

BILL. I wasn't too drunk to know where I woke up.

TOM. I see.

JULIE. *(Who has been listening bemused.)* Just a minute.

TOM. What do *you* want?

JULIE. Do I gather from all this that this is your real girl-friend?

TOM. Yes.

JULIE. The one who wasn't at home last night?

TOM. Yes.

JULIE. The one the 'big moment' was going to happen to?

JUDY. The what?

TOM. *(Awkward.)* Er... well, yes.

JULIE. *(Looking at BILL.)* Bloody hell!

BILL. *(Apprehensively.)* Now, Julie...

JULIE. You lot are like rabbits!

TOM. What?

BILL. Julie, please don't say anything I might regret.

TOM. You might regret?

BILL. *She* might regret.

TOM. Why should she? She doesn't know anything about this.

JULIE. On the contrary—I know a lot more about it than you know!

BILL. Julie...

TOM. What do you know?

JULIE. I'm not telling what I know. But if you knew what I know, I know one thing.

TOM. What?

JULIE. You wouldn't *want* to know!

TOM. What the hell are you blathering about?

BILL. Julie, will you belt up!

JULIE. Why should I belt up?

BILL. There are some things it's better people *don't* know at a time like this.

JULIE. Not at all—it's a time like this that people ought to know some things.

TOM. What things?

JULIE. They ought to know what they're getting themselves into before it's to late to get themselves out!

TOM. What? Who's getting themselves into what?

BILL. *(To JULIE.)* You're getting yourself into something you won't be able to finish.

JULIE. Whatever I may be getting into, he's getting himself into something a lot worse, and it's not half as bad as that poor girl in there is getting herself into!

TOM. I'm going out of my mind! Why is everyone talking gibberish?

(Next door, RACHEL has heard the shouting and comes through to investigate.)

RACHEL. What's going on in here?

BILL. Oh, Lord!

RACHEL. What's all the shouting about.

JULIE. You may well ask!

RACHEL. I am asking.

TOM. Something's been happening here, Rachel, which everyone seems to understand except you and I!

RACHEL. What? What's been happening?

TOM. I don't know. *(Indicates JULIE.)* Ask her.

RACHEL. *(To JULIE.)* What's been happening?

JULIE. (Indicating BILL.) Ask him.

RACHEL (*To BILL)* What's been happening?

BILL. *(Indicating JUDY.)* Ask her.

RACHEL. The chambermaid? What does she know about it?

JULIE. You may well ask!

RACHEL. *(Imperious.)* I *am* asking! *(To JUDY.)* Well?

JUDY. *(In agony.)* Um... I... um...

(There is a knock on the door. They all turn to look at it. It opens and RACHEL's mother, DAPHNE, enters, wearing an over-the-top outfit and hat, and carrying a splendid wedding dress.)

DAPHNE. Hello everyone—I'm here!

RACHEL. Mother!

DAPHNE. Isn't this wonderful! It's going to be the perfect wedding!

(RACHEL and TOM glare at her. BILL groans and collapses onto the sofa. JUDY bursts into tears.)

END OF ACT I

ACT II

(A few moments later. Everyone is talking at once.)

DAPHNE. I don't understand! What was it I did? All I said was that I wanted it to be a lovely wedding... (Etc.)

RACHEL. I want to know just what is going on here. Everyone has been behaving like idiots since I arrived, and... (Etc.)

TOM. There is something very peculiar happening here and I want to know what it is! Why will no one give me a straight answer to a straight question... ? (Etc.)

JULIE. I've never met such a bunch in my life! How you conduct your personal affairs is your own business, but really... (Etc.)

BILL. I don't know how I got myself into this situation. My whole world is crumbling about my head, and I... (Etc.)

JUDY. There's really nothing to make such a fuss about, honestly! I don't know why everyone is getting so worked up. It was just simply that... (Etc.)

(RACHEL puts her fingers in her mouth and produces an ear-splitting whistle. The noise stops.)

RACHEL. (Peremptorily.) Right—you *(Points at BILL)*, and you *(Points at TOM)*—in here! *(RACHEL opens the connecting*

57

door. They obediently go through to the bedroom. She follows and closes the door. The others crowd to the other side of the door to listen.) Now—just what is this all about? Tom?

TOM. Well, I er... *(To BILL.)* You tell her.

BILL. Well, I er...

RACHEL. I am not going to leave for this wedding until I find out what is going on, and why everyone is in such a neurotic state this morning!

BILL. Well you see, darling, it's like this. Tom has got himself into a bit of a fix...

TOM. *I've* got myself in a fix!

BILL. That girl who was in here...

RACHEL. Which girl?

BILL. Judy... er, Julie—isn't actually the chambermaid.

RACHEL. Who is she?

BILL. She's Tom's girlfriend.

TOM. Thank you.

RACHEL. I thought the other one was his girlfriend.

BILL. She is. She's his other girlfriend.

RACHEL. What?

TOM. Thank you very much.

BILL. As you know, he got a bit confused about which of his girlfriends was turning up for the wedding. Well, they both have.

RACHEL. Oh my goodness! *(To TOM.)* How did that happen?

TOM. Well, it, er... they, er... I, er...

BILL. He had only just broken up with one, you see...

RACHEL. *(To TOM.)* Which one?

TOM. Er... this one... that one...

BILL. Judy... no—Julie...

RACHEL. Make up your minds!

BILL. Julie. *(To TOM.)* Wasn't it?

TOM. Yes, Julie. Definitely.

BILL. Definitely Julie.

RACHEL. Why?

BILL. Why what?

RACHEL. Why did you break up with her?

TOM. Because, er...

BILL. Because he met Julie... er, Judy.

TOM. Yes.

RACHEL. Ah.

BILL. And he fell so head over heels for Judy that he asked her down for the wedding, forgetting that he'd already asked Julie. And now they've both turned up together. And he's caught with his trousers down... so to speak.

TOM. *(Derisive.)* Hah!

RACHEL. What?

TOM. Nothing.

RACHEL. So why was Julie pretending to be the chambermaid when I met her?

TOM. Because, er...

BILL. Because she'd found out about Judy, and being a frightfully good sport she accepted the situation, and agreed to pretend to be the chambermaid so that Judy wouldn't realize who she was.

TOM. Yes.

RACHEL. I see. Well, I must say, Tom, you love life seems to be in as big a mess as ever.

TOM. Yes—doesn't it?

(TOM glowers at BILL.)

RACHEL. I always thought you were so competent—why can't you get that right?

TOM. I, er... well...

RACHEL. What are you going to do about them both?

TOM. Good question. *(Pointedly.)* What do you suggest, Bill?

BILL. I suggest that, er... well, I suggest you should have a serious think about which one of them you want, and which one you don't want, and then go to the one you don't want, and tell her you don't want her, and then—with any luck— *(Pointedly.)* you'll end up with the one you want.

RACHEL. I thought he knew which one he wanted.

BILL. Ah, well I'm not so sure that he does. That's why he's in such a mess. It's a Freudian dilemma.

RACHEL. His whole life seems to be a Freudian dilemma. Well hurry up and resolve it, will you, Tom. We do have a little matter of a wedding to get on with.

TOM. Right.

RACHEL. But if you want my advice, I'd think twice about getting too involved with Judy.

TOM. Why?

RACHEL. Her sensitivity leaves something to be desired. She insisted on giving me advice about my choice of a husband—on the day I'm about to marry him!

TOM. *(Glaring at BILL.)* Are you sure it was bad advice?

BILL. *(Glaring back.)* Watch it!

RACHEL. Anyway, can you organize your amorous affairs next door?

TOM. Right.

RACHEL. And I meanwhile would like to organize my wedding dress. Will you ask Mother to bring it through? *(DAPHNE, listening at the door, goes to get the dress. RACHEL sees BILL staring at her curiously.)* What are you staring at?

BILL. I've never seen you like this.

RACHEL. Like what?

BILL. So... commanding.

RACHEL. Well someone has to take command here, or our married life is going to start in chaos.

BILL. Yes.

RACHEL. *(Dismissing him with a wave.)* Run along both of you.

BILL & TOM. *(Together.)* Right.

(BILL and TOM go through to the reception room. TOM picks up the toilet brush, as he goes.)

TOM. I'll give you Freudian dilemma!

(DAPHNE hurries past them with the dress.)

DAPHNE. *(Flustering.)* Have you sorted everything out, boys?
BILL. Yes.
TOM. I'm just going to sort him out now.
DAPHNE. You do look as if you need it, Bill. You haven't
even shaved yet!
BILL. I've been a bit busy.
DAPHNE. Oh dear. *(Going through.)* Rachel, there seems
to be so much going on, and so many people around. Your
father's arriving soon, and you know how furious he gets if
things aren't organized.
RACHEL It will be all right, Mother. I'm going to have a
bath now. Have you taken up the hem on the dress?
DAPHNE. I just want to make the final adjustments when
it's on.

*(RACHEL goes into the bathroom. DAPHNE unwraps the
dress, and takes out needle and cotton.)*

DAPHNE. *(Singing to herself in a piercing contralto.)* Here
comes the bride...

*(Next door TOM closes the connecting door against the sound,
and glares at the other three.)*

TOM. Right—now I'm going to get to the bottom of this.
JULIE. Yes, I think you should.
TOM. Just what is going on here?
BILL. Well, er...
JUDY. Tom—perhaps I'd better have a word with you.
JULIE. Yes, perhaps you'd better.
BILL. *(Nervous.)* Now, Judy...
JUDY. Perhaps, Bill, it should be in private.
JULIE. Yes, perhaps it should.
BILL. Judy, please...

TOM. Belt up, you!

JULIE. About time.

TOM. And you too!

JULIE. Well!

TOM. *(Waving the toilet brush.)* Mind your own business for once, and get on with your proper job!

JULIE. *(Outraged.)* After all I've done to help!

TOM. *(To BILL.)* You, go and get ready for your wedding— if you've got time to fit it in with all your other activities.

BILL. Right. *(With an apprehensive look at JUDY.)* Be careful what you say. You don't want to spoil a beautiful relationship.

TOM. Whose?

BILL. Yours and hers of course.

JULIE. Hah!

TOM. Out!

(He pushes BILL and JULIE out of the door.)

DAPHNE. *(Next door, singing.)* ... all dressed in white...

(TOM turns to JUDY, who has taken off the overall.)

TOM. Well?

JUDY. Promise not to lose your temper.

TOM. I never lose my temper.

JUDY. You see, what happened was this. After you and I had that row last night, I began to have serious doubts about us.

TOM. About us?

JUDY. Oh, it wasn't just the stupid old stag night. I understood about that. It was just that we don't seem to... well, click—do we?

TOM. Click?

JUDY. Gel.

TOM. That's what this week-end was for.

JUDY. I know it was intended to be... our big moment...

TOM. Yes.

JUDY. But, well... after our big row I was left with a small feeling that our big moment mightn't turn out quite so big after all. So I'm afraid I decided to call if off and go home.

TOM. Just because of a silly argument?

JUDY. I'm sorry. I came here to tell you.

TOM. There's more to it than that. You don't just rush off in a tiff because of a huff... a huff because of a tiff.

JUDY. I was going to take the train actually.

TOM. Oh for God's sake... !

JUDY. Sorry.

TOM. There's something else. Tell me.

JUDY. Well all right—yes, there is.

TOM. What?

JUDY. *(Hesitating.)* Oh dear...

TOM. *Tell* me.

JUDY. Even if the moment hadn't turned out quite as big as we'd hoped, I might have settled for a fairly small moment... except that something got in the way.

TOM. What?

JUDY. Another man.

TOM. Another man?

JUDY. Yes.

TOM. *(Exploding.)* Who is he? I'll kill him!

JUDY. You said you never lose your temper.

TOM. *(Controlling himself.)* All right, I'm calm, I'm calm. What happened?

JUDY. When I couldn't find you here—I was wondering what to do when, quite by accident, I met this man.

TOM. Here?

JUDY. Yes.

TOM. In the hotel?

JUDY. Yes.

TOM. *(Waving the toilet brush.)* I'll kill him!

JUDY. *(Taking it from him.)* I can't explain if you're going to be like that.

TOM. All right, I'm calm. What happened?

JUDY. What happened was that the small moment I might have had with you turned out to be a big moment with him instead.

TOM. Are you saying what I think you're saying?

JUDY. I'm saying that, for the first time in my life, I was bowled over. Call it love at first sight if you like. I didn't mean to—it just came out of the blue.

DAPHNE. *(Next door.)* ... Here comes the bride...

(TOM and JUDY try to ignore the sound.)

JUDY. And, I'm afraid it rather scuppered whatever might have happened between you and me.

TOM. Let me get this straight—are you telling me that last night you shared that bedroom with a man you'd only just met?

(TOM points across the passage.)

JUDY. No.

TOM. Swear?

JUDY. Cross my heart.

TOM. Well that's something at least. So who is this swine?

JUDY. Oh, he's not a swine. He's really very nice.

TOM. Nobody nice goes around pinching other people's girlfriends!

JUDY. He didn't pinch me. I told you, it was pure chance.

TOM. So who is he?

JUDY. No-one special-just a man. You'd like him.

TOM. How do you know?

JUDY. You have a lot in common.

TOM. Did Bill meet him?

JUDY. *(Quickly.)* No, no! They never met face to face.

TOM. So did you meet him looking for his room key on the landing too?

JUDY. Er... no.

TOM. Where then?

JUDY. In the bar.

TOM. We were in the bar. Having our stag party.

JUDY. It was after the party was over. That's why I couldn't find you.

TOM. So he picked you up in the bar!

JUDY. I picked him up actually. He was very drunk and was having trouble standing.

TOM. You fell for a drunk?

JUDY. Well he fell first—off his bar stool.

TOM. Terrific. Very romantic. Does he feel the same way about you?

JUDY. Probably not, no. He just needed a shoulder to cry on. He's rather tied up elsewhere, you see.

TOM. You mean he's married?

JUDY. More or less.

TOM. The swine! I'll kill him! Does he know how you feel about him?

JUDY. No.

TOM. Why not?

JUDY. I didn't feel I should tell him, in the circumstances.

TOM. But you feel it's fair to tell me?

JUDY. It's only right you know where you stand.

TOM. Knee deep in manure by the sound of it.

(JUDY touches TOM sympathetically.)

JUDY. If you think about it, Tom, it wouldn't have been that big a moment, would it?

TOM. *(Forlorn.)* I don't seem to be cut out for big moments with anyone.

JUDY. You'll find someone.

TOM. Well you can tell your lover boy that, when I find out who he is, I won't kill him.

JUDY. Good.

TOM. I'll just cut off his dip-stick with a carving knife.

JUDY. No—please Tom!

TOM. Why? Spoil *your* big moment, would it?

JUDY. Look, I seem to have cause enough trouble round here today. I'd better leave.

DAPHNE. *(Next door.)* ... Here comes the bride, all dressed in white... *(She comes through with the wedding dress.)* Oh. Are you still trying to sort yourselves out?

JUDY. We've done that. I was just...

DAPHNE. Ah, well you're the very person I need. I've been taking the hem up on Rachel's dress, and I'm not sure if I've done it evenly. Can I ask you to try it on for me while she's in the bath?

JUDY. Oh, well I was just about to...

DAPHNE. It won't take a moment.

JUDY. Well, I...

DAPHNE. It's so important we have it right.

JUDY. But I...

DAPHNE. *Please.*

JUDY. *(Reluctantly.)* Oh, well all right...

DAPHNE. Thank you. *(Ushers her into the bedroom.)* Come in here. *(To TOM.)* You can have her back in a moment.

TOM. Thank you very much.

DAPHNE. *(Turning in the doorway.)* I do hope this is *the* one this time, Tom. It's high time you settled down.

(DAPHNE goes into the bedroom where JUDY starts to slip out of her dress and into the wedding dress. TOM paces next door growling with fury. BILL enters in his wedding trousers, struggling with the collar of a stiff shirt.)

BILL. Oh Tom, thank heavens! What's happened? Where is everyone?

TOM. Next door.

BILL. Is, er ... is everything all right?

TOM. Absolutely wonderful!

BILL. Oh, good. Give me a hand with this damned collar, will you? I haven't worn one of these since my confirmation day.

TOM. Come here! *(TOM takes hold of BILL's collar, fiddles for a second, then loses his temper and roars with rage.)* Rrrraaagh!

(TOM grips the collar ends in his fury, almost throttling BILL.)

BILL. Gggggg!

TOM. I'm going to cut it off with a carving knife!

BILL. Gggggg!

(BILL sinks to his knees, purple in the face.)

TOM. I'm going to do unmentionable things!

BILL. *(Hoarse.)* For God's sake... !

TOM. By the time I've finished there aren't going to be any more big moments for anybody! Do you hear me?

BILL. Please ... please ...

(TOM releases him. He collapses on the floor in a heap.)

TOM. *(Pacing.)* I've never been so angry in my life!

BILL. *(In a hoarse whisper.)* What's happened?

TOM. I've found out what was going on here last night, that's what's happened.

BILL. You found out?

TOM. Yes No wonder Judy was behaving so strangely! Bastard!

BILL. Now steady on!

TOM. To calmly step in and steal her from under my nose like that!

BILL. It wasn't like that.

TOM. To take advantage of her, just because we'd had a little tiff over nothing!

BILL. That's not how it was at all.

TOM. I tell you, I'm going to ... What?

BILL. You've got it all wrong.

TOM. I've got what wrong.

BILL. What you're talking about.

TOM. How do you know what I'm talking about?

BILL. Well, because ... What *are* you talking about?

TOM. I'm talking about Judy—that's what I'm talking about.

BILL. That's what I'm talking about.

TOM. How can you be talking about it? You don't know about it.

BILL. Don't I?

TOM. What do you know?

BILL. What do *you* know?

TOM. She's been seduced by another man—that's what I know.

BILL. Another man?

TOM. Yes. Some bastard caught her at a vulnerable moment and stole her affections. And when I find out who it is I'm going to cut off his dip-stick with a carving knife!

BILL. When you find out?

TOM. A blunt one!

BILL. But you haven't found out yet?

TOM. No. But when I do...

BILL. Thank God for that!

TOM. What d'you mean?

BILL. I mean thank God you haven't done anything like that—on my wedding day.

TOM. What do you know about it anyway?

BILL. Me?

TOM. You said it wasn't like that.

BILL. She, er... told me it wasn't like that.

TOM. She told you about it?

BILL. Yes.

TOM. When?

BILL. When she found me last night.

TOM. On the landing?

BILL. Yes, on the landing.

TOM. What did she tell you?

BILL. She told me ... What did she tell you?

TOM. She told me she met this other man in the hotel here last night.

BILL. Yes, that's what she told me.

TOM. And she told me he was plastered and in a bad way over his situation, and they both cried on each other's shoulders, and evidently consoled each other no end!

BILL. Yes, that's what she told me.

TOM. And she told me the big moment with me was off, because it was such a big moment with him.

BILL. Yes, that's what ... She what?

TOM. In fact it seems it was practically the biggest moment in history, with the biggest bastard in history, which leaves me feeling the biggest schmuck in history!

BILL. Really?

TOM. And when I find him I'm going to give him the biggest vasectomy in history!

BILL. She said that? It was the biggest moment in history?

TOM. Love at first sight, she called it. A feeling she'd never had for anyone before. Why can't something like that ever happen to me?

BILL. Is that really what she said? Love at first sight?

TOM. While the swine was so drunk he fell off his bar stool! Some women have a very peculiar sense of timing.

BILL. Where is she now?

TOM. Why do you want to know?

BILL. I think I ought to talk to her about this.

TOM. Why do you want to talk to her? You've got your own matters to worry about.

BILL. Yes, but I ... well I wouldn't want a distraction like this hanging over my wedding day. Where is she?

TOM. It's his wedding day that's going to suffer when I find him!

BILL. No, no—you mustn't do anything like that. Where is she? Has she gone?

TOM. Never mind where she is. You get on and...

(At that moment DAPHNE opens the communicating door.)

DAPHNE. *(Singing.)*Here comes the bride, all dressed in white... *(Ushers JUDY in, dressed in the wedding gown.)* Well, how does it look?

(It looks stunning. The two men stare at her.)

BILL. *(Who is closest to her.)* Judy... !
DAPHNE. Is the hem level, do you think?
BILL. *(In almost a whisper.)* Oh my God!
DAPHNE. What? What's wrong?
BILL. You look ...

(BILL tails off, speechless.)

DAPHNE. *(Fussing round the dress.)* It's all right, isn't it?

TOM. *(Stepping between BILL and JUDY.)* Here—this isn't on, you know. You shouldn't be seeing the dress before the church.

DAPHNE. *(Dismayed.)* Oh, no, I forgot! Of course you shouldn't, Bill! I didn't realize you were in here.

BILL. *(Still dumb-struck.)* I...

DAPHNE. Rachel will never forgive me! Quickly—come back in here!

(DAPHNE urges JUDY back into the bedroom.)

BILL. Judy ...!
JUDY. *(Stopping.)* Yes?
BILL. We... we must ...
JUDY. No, Bill. You must get ready for your wedding.

(JUDY goes through with DAPHNE fussing round the dress.)

DAPHNE. I just need to put a few stitches in now.

(The two men are left on their own again.)

TOM. God, didn't she look stunning?
BILL. *(Nodding dumbly.)* Mmm.
TOM. What I wouldn't give to take her down the aisle look-
ing like that!
BILL. Mmm.
TOM. And instead, some other swine's gone and pinched
her. *(Sitting.)* I think I'll kill myself.
BILL. *(Sitting beside him.)* I'll join you.
TOM. Right. *(Pause.)* Why? You've got what you want.
BILL. Oh, yes. I forgot.
TOM. Haven't you?
BILL. Yes. It's my hangover.

(TOM and BILL sit in gloomy silence.)

DAPHNE. *(Next door.)* ... all dressed in white... la la la-
la... here comes the bride...

(The reception room door opens and JULIE enters.)

JULIE. I thought I ought to... *(Stares at their gloomy faces.)*
What's happened? Is it a funeral now?
TOM. What do you want?
JULIE. I thought I should tell you that there's a large red-
faced man down in the lobby who's causing quite a lot of

trouble. Would it be the bride's father?

TOM. Gerald! Yes, it probably is. What's he doing?

JULIE. He's demanding to know why all the reception arrangements aren't ready.

TOM. Oh God—I haven't done the table plans!

JULIE He's ordering the staff about like a sergeant major. So far he's provoked the resignation of the head waiter, two hall porters and half the kitchen staff. I'm practically the only one left.

BILL. Go and sort it out, Tom.

TOM. I'm going to sort out this bastard first!

BILL. Please!

TOM. I thought weddings were supposed to be fun!

(Hurries out of the door. JULIE goes to follow.)

BILL. Julie—just a moment.

JULIE. What?

BILL. I need your help.

JULIE. Oh, no! I've done enough helping for one day.

BILL. Please, Julie. It's a matter of life and death.

JULIE. Whose?

BILL. Mine.

JULIE. Well you deserve to die—a very nasty death! Bonking your best friend's girlfriend, on your own wedding day!

BILL. You don't understand, Julie. It wasn't what it seemed.

JULIE. What was it then—sex therapy?

BILL. Julie, just take my word for it—I need your help if today isn't going to end up as the biggest disaster in the history of weddings.

JULIE. It's well on the way. What do you want?

BILL. I want a moment in private with Judy.

JULIE. His girlfriend?

BILL. Yes.

JULIE. The call girl.

BILL. She's not a call girl.

JULIE. She was behaving like a call girl.

BILL. No, she ... *please*, Julie!

JULIE. What do you want me to do?

BILL. She's next door with my fiancee's mother. I want you to get the mother out of there so I can have a word with her.

JULIE. How many letters in it?

BILL. Julie! *(Urging her towards the communicating door.)* I'll hide until you've got rid of her.

JULIE. What do I say?

BILL. Say her husband's creating havoc downstairs.

JULIE. While you're creating havoc upstairs.

BILL. Please!

(BILL opens the door and pushes her through. He then crosses the reception room and goes out to the corridor, closing the door behind him.)

JULIE. Er ... excuse me.

DAPHNE. Yes?

JULIE. There's a gentleman downstairs in the lobby who I believe is your husband...

DAPHNE. Gerald?

JULIE. He rather urgently needs to see you about the reception arrangements.

DAPHNE. Tom is supposed to be dealing with those!

JULIE. Well, he does seem to be making a bit of a commotion down there.

DAPHNE. Oh, trust Gerald! We should have left him at home. *(To JUDY.)* I'm sorry dear. It's nearly finished. Can you just hold on for a minute or two while I see what's going on.

JUDY. Well, I...

DAPHNE. I'll be straight back.

(DAPHNE hurries through the connecting door, and exits via the reception room.)

JULIE. Very nice, you look. Who exactly is supposed to be getting married here?

JUDY. I'm just trying it on.

JULIE. Yes, you're good at trying it on, aren't you?

JUDY. Now look here...

JULIE. Well, don't go away. There's someone else who wants to try it on with you as well.

JUDY. What?

JULIE. Don't ask me what he wants, but if I were you I'd be very careful before you say 'I do'.

(JULIE follows DAPHNE out. As the connecting door closes, the passage door to the bedroom opens. BILL enters.)

JUDY. Bill!

BILL. Shhh! *(Whispers.)* Is Rachel still in there?

JUDY. Yes.

BILL. *(Taking JUDY by the hand.)* Quick! Come in here.

(Leads her into the reception room which JULIE has just left, and closes the door.)

JUDY. What's happening?

BILL. That's what I want to find out.

JUDY. What do you mean?

(Sits her on the sofa and sits beside her.)

BILL. What happened last night, Judy?

JUDY. You know what happened.

BILL. I don't mean just what happened in bed...

JUDY. Oh, you do remember that much then?

BILL. Only too well.

JUDY. Ah.

BILL. Tell me it meant nothing, Judy. Tell me it was just... chemistry.

JUDY. Probably.

BILL. That's all it was, wasn't it?

JUDY. Yes.

BILL. So how did we get there?

JUDY. To bed?

BILL. *Why* did we get there?

JUDY. You don't remember that?

BILL. I remember some of it—on my side. I want to know what happened on your side.

JUDY. We changed sides quite a lot actually.

BILL. *(Desperate.)* This is no time for jokes, Judy!

JUDY. It's over. Why does it matter?

BILL. Because... of something Tom just told me.

JUDY. What?

BILL. He told me... that you told him... it was a big moment.

JUDY. Oh.

BILL. Possibly the biggest moment of your life.

JUDY. I see.

BILL. Was it, Judy? I need to know because I'm about to take the biggest step of *my* life.

JUDY. Well, whatever it was, it can't change that now, can it?

BILL. I don't know, but... What happened exactly? How did we meet? Tell me!

JUDY. All right. I got to the hotel quite late, and I found that the stag party had broken up and everyone had gone home. The only people around were one sozzled man in the bar, and the night porter who was plying him with brandies.

BILL. George?

JUDY. Into which he was weeping steadily, in between verses of 'You Give Me Fever'. Very out of tune.

BILL. Why was I still in the bar?

JUDY. George said he'd taken you up to your room, but then five minutes later you'd come downstairs again... or rather fallen downstairs again... and demanded a drink because there was no way you could sleep in the circumstances.

BILL. What circumstances?

JUDY. He said you'd said your mind was in a complete turmoil because you didn't know if you were doing the right thing.

BILL. What thing?

JUDY. Getting married.

BILL. I said that?

JUDY. That's what George said you said.

BILL. And what did you say?

JUDY. I sat down beside you, and said my mind was in a bit of a turmoil too, and could I have a brandy too, and so George left us with the brandy bottle and went back to his desk.

BILL. Did I know who you were?

JUDY. No.

BILL. Why not?

JUDY. I didn't want to tell you. I wasn't sure whether I should have come on this trip in any case.

BILL. So what happened?

JUDY. Well you poured out your heart to me, and said you didn't really know if the girl you were marrying was the right girl for you, and you were just marrying her because everyone had always said she was the right girl for you...

BILL. I said that?

JUDY. And I poured out my heart to you, and said I knew the man I was visiting was the wrong man for me, but that I'd agreed to spend the weekend with him because I was tired of looking for the right man for me...

BILL. Was that true?

JUDY. Yes. And then...

BILL. Then what?

JUDY. You fell off your bar stool.

BILL. *(Hopelessly.)* Typical.

JUDY. You'd hit your head and were half-concussed. So I picked you up, and helped you upstairs to your room. Then as I was trying to hold you up outside your door, and find your key at the same time, you said...

BILL. What?

JUDY. You said you knew who was the right girl for you.

BILL. Who?

JUDY. Me. Well, of course I knew you were drunk, and didn't really mean it, but you said that there was only one way to find out if you really meant it, and that was...

BILL. How?

JUDY. To kiss me.

BILL. So?

JUDY. So you did.

BILL. And?

JUDY. I shouldn't be telling you this.

BILL. You have to.

JUDY. Well, I don't know if it told you anything, but it certainly told me something.

BILL. What?

JUDY. I went weaker at the knees than you were. In fact it miraculously seemed to sober you up, and I suddenly found myself being carried into the bedroom. And I thought I shouldn't be doing this. And then you kissed me again and I thought I couldn't *help* doing this. And then you began to take my clothes off, and I thought I definitely shouldn't be doing this. And then you kissed me in a few other places, and I thought I'd like to do this for ever. And then... well you know the rest.

BILL. Oh my God.

JUDY. You remember now?

BILL. I thought it was a dream.

JUDY. A lovely dream.

BILL. What are we going to do?

JUDY. There's nothing we can do. Your fiancee's next door getting ready for your wedding, and a hundred people are gathering in the church across the green, and you're flying to Jamaica in the morning, and...

(JUDY bursts into tears.)

BILL. Judy, Judy...
JUDY. Oh, Bill...

(BILL and JUDY cling to each other.)

BILL. Kiss me.
JUDY. (Standing.) We mustn't.
BILL. *(Standing.)* No.
JUDY. *(Turning to him.)* Kiss me.

*(BILL and JUDY kiss. Next door RACHEL emerges from the
bathroom, wrapped in a bathrobe.)*

RACHEL. Mother? *(She crosses the room and opens the
connecting door.)* Mother? *(BILL instinctively drops to his
knees behind JUDY, and crawls behind the sofa. RACHEL
sees JUDY.)* Oh. You're still here?
JUDY. Yes.
RACHEL. What are you doing in my wedding dress?
JUDY. Trying it on.
RACHEL. What?
JUDY. Er... your mother asked me to try it on, to get the
hem right.
RACHEL. Oh.
JUDY. I'll, er ... take it off now.

*(JUDY heads for the bedroom. RACHEL follows. BILL crawls
frantically to the passage door. As he reaches it, it opens
and he vanishes behind it. A thunderous-looking TOM appears carrying a large carving knife.)*

TOM. Rachel?
RACHEL. *(Calling from the bedroom.)* Tom?

*(TOM closes the door and comes downstage. BILL has dropped
to his knees again, and crawls back to behind the sofa.*

RACHEL returns from the bedroom.)

TOM. Where's Judy?

JUDY. *(Also returning.)* Here.

TOM. I want to talk to you!

RACHEL. *(Staring at the knife.)* Where did you get that knife?

TOM. It's for cutting wedding cakes... and other things.

JUDY. Now, Tom...

TOM. Whilst I was downstairs trying to stop Rachel's father changing all the arrangements, and stop the staff resigning en masse, and stop the manager throwing us all out onto the street...

RACHEL. *(Furious.)* Oh God!

TOM. ... I happened to meet someone you know.

JUDY. Who?

TOM. George.

JUDY. George?

TOM. Yes, the night porter. Because of all the chaos going on down there, he's been roused from his slumbers and ordered to act as the day porter.

JUDY. So?

TOM. So I was able to ask him about last night, and what you told me happened last night, and about the other man you met here last night...

JUDY. And?

TOM. And he told me that, apart from Bill, there *was* no other man here last night.

JUDY. Did he?

TOM. So who *was* this other man last night?

(Behind their backs BILL is making another attempt to crawl to the door.)

RACHEL. Tom, do we really have to go into your affairs right now. You and Bill have to be at the church in half an hour.

TOM. Sorry, Rachel, but this is one affair I have to clear up. *(To JUDY.)* Well?

JUDY. Er...

(BILL gets to the door. Again it opens and he vanishes behind it. DAPHNE appears.)

DAPHNE. *(In a fluster.)* Oh, Rachel, what are we going to do?
RACHEL. *Now* what?
DAPHNE. It's bedlam downstairs! Your father's charging around like a madman, the staff are all on strike, and the manager's tearing his hair out! What's happened to our perfect wedding?
RACHEL. *(Decisively.)* Tom, I don't care what's happening in your love life right now. This is my wedding day, and you're the best man, and this is your responsibility! Do something about it!
TOM. *(Reluctantly.)* Right.
RACHEL. And do give them that knife back. We'd like to be about to cut the cake, if we ever get that far!
TOM. Right.

(BILL has crawled behind them all into the bedroom, where he heads for that *passage door. TOM goes to the reception room door. DAPHNE has gone to the window. RACHEL and JUDY go towards the bedroom.)*

DAPHNE. Oh, look—all the guests are flooding into the church. We're never going to be ready!

(BILL has reached the passage door just as it opens and once again he vanishes behind it. JULIE appears. RACHEL and JUDY come into the bedroom. TOM has left the reception room.)

JULIE. Ah.
RACHEL. What do *you* want?

JULIE. The hotel manager has sent me to say that some-one has to come and take the bride's father away before he brings the hotel to a standstill.

RACHEL. We know that already.

JULIE. I'm just delivering the message.

RACHEL. Why are *you* delivering it?

JULIE. Well, because I...

RACHEL. The manager shouldn't be involving guests in all this.

JULIE. He's run out of staff.

RACHEL. Oh, this is too much! Where's Bill? If he had any sort of gumption he'd be handling all this!

(BILL has at last managed to get into the doorway and stands there as if he has just entered.)

BILL. Hello? Did somebody want me?

RACHEL. Bill! There you are. What are you doing? You're still only half dressed!

BILL. I could say the same about you, darling.

RACHEL. I'm ready except for my dress. The only thing you look ready for is Halloween!

BILL. Well, I er...

(TOM appears behind BILL from the passage, with the knife.)

TOM. Aha! I thought it was you!

BILL. Oh God!

RACHEL. You're supposed to be going downstairs!

TOM. I am, I am. *(Threatening.)* But I need Bill's help.

RACHEL. Well take him away! Take everyone away and sort things out! I want to get dressed!

TOM. Right. *(To BILL and JULIE.)* You and you—in there.

(TOM herds BILL and JULIE back to the reception room wav-ing the knife. Shuts the door behind him.)

RACHEL. Thank heavens. *(To JUDY.)* May I have my dress, please.

JUDY. Yes.

(JUDY starts to take the dress off with DAPHNE's help.)

TOM. *(Next door.)* Now then—let's get to the bottom of this!

BILL. *(Looking at the knife.)* What's that for?

TOM. I've told you what it's for.

BILL. You weren't serious!

JULIE. What was it for?

TOM. Mind your own business!

JULIE. Ooo! I've never met such a rude lot in my life!

TOM. Look, we've finished with your services. Go and make up some beds or something!

JULIE. Charming! Well as a matter of interest there aren't any beds left to make up.

TOM. Yes there are—there's the bedroom over there.

(TOM points across the passage.)

JULIE. No, there aren't. No one has slept in the bedroom over there.

BILL. Julie...

TOM. Yes, they have—Judy slept in it.

JULIE. I know which bedrooms have been slept in and which haven't.

(JULIE goes to the door.)

TOM. What?

BILL. *(Desperate.)* Julie...

JULIE. This one has, and that one hasn't!

(JULIE goes out. Deathly silence.)

TOM. *(Menacing.)* What did that mean?

BILL. Now, Tom...

TOM. I think I'm finally beginning to see the light.

BILL. *(Picking up the toilet brush from where JUDY has left it.)* No, I don't think so.

TOM. *(Advancing slowly with the knife.)* Judy's fallen for another man...

BILL. *(Retreating and holding up the toilet brush.)* Another man somewhere else.

TOM. You spent the night with some girl you'd never met before...

BILL. A call girl who's left... gone...

TOM. *(Still advancing.)* Judy spent the night in a bed other than that one...

BILL. Not this one. Another one... another one...

TOM. *(Stopping.)* Tell me one thing then.

BILL. What?

TOM. How did you get that bump on the back of your head?

BILL. *(Puzzled.)* This bump?

TOM. Yes.

BILL. I fell off a bar stool. *(With a roar of range TOM goes for him.)* No—no—please...

(TOM chases BILL round the sofa with the knife.)

TOM. I'll cut it off! I swear it—I'll cut it off!

(BILL makes it to the connecting door, and dashes through. The girls are both half into their respective dresses.)

RACHEL & JUDY. *(Together.)* Do you mind!

BILL. Sorry, I er...

(TOM comes storming through the door with another roar. BILL throws the toilet brush at him and dashes out through the passage door.)

RACHEL & JUDY. *(Together.)* Do you mind!

TOM. Sorry, I... *(Seeing JUDY.)* You! You... you... traitor!

(JUDY grabs her things and heads for the bathroom.)

JUDY. I'll dress in here.

(JUDY vanishes.)

RACHEL. Tom! What on earth is it *now*!

TOM. I'm going to ruin his marriage prospects for evermore—that's what!

RACHEL. Why?

DAPHNE. What's he done?

TOM. You may well ask!

RACHEL. I *am* asking!

DAPHNE. So'm I.

TOM. I haven't time now—I'll tell you later! *(Dashes to the door, then stops.)* No, I won't. I'll tell you now!

RACHEL. What?

DAPHNE. Yes, what?

TOM. You jolly well have a right to know too.

RACHEL. Know what?

DAPHNE. Know what?

TOM. Sorry about this, Daphne. But as her oldest friend I feel it's my duty to give Rachel some painful news.

DAPHNE. What?

RACHEL. Yes, what?

TOM. I think you'd better sit down.

RACHEL. *(Crossly.)* What *is* it?

DAPHNE. *(Beside herself.)* Yes, what *is* it??

TOM. Your betrothed—who you thought was sleeping alone over there last night—while I was sleeping with my girlfriend in here last night—and who I also thought was sleeping alone over there last night—until I arrived here this morning—because I *wasn't* actually sleeping in here last night—

I have discovered *wasn't* sleeping alone over there at all last night—but was actually sleeping in here last night—with my girlfriend, who *I* was supposed to be sleeping with last night!

(Pause.)

RACHEL. What?
DAPHNE. What?
TOM. That's right.
RACHEL. Bill spend last night in here?
TOM. Yes.
RACHEL. With your girlfriend?
TOM. Yes.
RACHEL. In the same bed?
TOM. Yes.
DAPHNE. Which girlfriend?
TOM *(Pointing at the bathroom.) The* girlfriend. Judy.
RACHEL. That's Julie.
TOM. That's... Ah yes. I get them confused.
RACHEL. So which do you really mean—Julie or Judy?
TOM. I *really* mean Judy!
RACHEL. Bill slept here—with Judy—last night?
   TOM. Exactly. Now, if you'll excuse me, you have a wedding to go to, and I have a dip-stick to cut off.

(TOM dashes out of the door with the knife. Pause. The two women stare at each other.)

RACHEL. *(Bursting into tears.)* Mummy!
DAPHNE. *(Holding her.)* There, there, darling.
RACHEL. I *knew* something was wrong!
DAPHNE. Never mind.
RACHEL. How could he do this to me?
DAPHNE. Men! They're all alike.
RACHEL. What am I going to do?
DAPHNE. I don't know.

RACHEL. Everyone's waiting at the church!

DAPHNE. *(Pause.)* Is there anyone else you'd like to marry?

(RACHEL bursts into tears again. JULIE enters from the passage.)

JULIE. I'm sorry to bother you again, but the manager says that if you don't get your father out of the hotel, and sort out the seating for the tables, and stop the best man running around with a carving knife, he's going to cancel the entire reception, and you'll have to hold it on the village green. *(Pause. The other two stare at her. JULIE shuffles awkwardly.)* Er... that's what he told me to tell you, which is why I'm telling you.

RACHEL. *(Dangerous.)* You're Judy, right?

JULIE. *(Apprehensive.)* Am I?

RACHEL. You must know if you are or not?

JULIE. Yes, I am.

RACHEL. Would you leave us alone, please, Mother? I'd like a little word with Judy in private.

DAPHNE. You won't do anything rash, will you, dear?

RACHEL. Don't worry. Go and placate Father, and don't under any circumstances let him up here. I've got enough to deal with.

DAPHNE. Right, dear. *(Shakes her head.)* We should have left him at home.

(As DAPHNE goes out, BILL enters the room next door, looking even more dishevelled. Both doors close together. BILL leans breathlessly against his door. RACHEL picks up the toilet brush and turns menacingly to JULIE.)

RACHEL. Right.

JULIE. What did she mean—rash?

RACHEL. It all makes sense now.

JULIE. What?

RACHEL. You've been out to ruin my marriage right from the start!

JULIE. Me? I've been trying to save your marriage!

RACHEL. You've a funny way of showing it!

JULIE. Well it's a pretty funny marriage.

RACHEL. How dare you! Who are you to judge my personal relationships? But now I know what it's all about.

JULIE. What?

RACHEL. Jealousy!

JULIE. Eh?

RACHEL. You want him for yourself!

JULIE. Who? What are you talking about?

RACHEL. You didn't spend the night with Tom at all, did you?

JULIE. Well, I er...

RACHEL. You spent it with Bill!

JULIE. Did I?

RACHEL. The nerve of it! On the night before my wedding!

JULIE.. I thought I spent it with Tom?

RACHEL. You mean you don't *know* who you spent it with?

JULIE. That's who I'm *supposed* to have spent it with.

RACHEL. So did you, or didn't you?

JULIE. No, I didn't.

RACHEL. There you are then!

JULIE. But just because I didn't spend it with Tom doesn't mean I spent it with Bill!

RACHEL. Tom says you did.

JULIE. *Tom* says I did?

RACHEL. Yes.

JULIE. When?

RACHEL. Just now.

JULIE. Just now?

RACHEL. Do stop repeating everything I say!

JULIE. What did he say exactly?

RACHEL. He said that all the time he was supposed to be

in here with you, Judy, he was actually somewhere else altogether, and it was *Bill* who was in here with you, Judy!

JULIE. Ah—I get it now!

RACHEL. No, you got it last night. *(Advances with the toilet brush.)* And I'm going to see you don't get it again!

JULIE. No, no! *(Backing away.)* Look, you've got this all wrong.

RACHEL. *(Advancing.)* Oh, no I haven't.

JULIE. Please—just let me explain!

RACHEL. *(Stopping.)* Very well—explain.

JULIE. You see, what happened was... *(Pause.)* It's too complicated.

(JULIE makes a dash for the connecting door with RACHEL in hot pursuit. They go through it and come face to face with BILL.)

BILL. Ah.

JULIE. *(Getting behind him.)* Here he is—ask him!

RACHEL. Very well. Bill?

BILL. *(Apprehensive.)* Yes?

RACHEL. You know I can always tell when you're lying, don't you, Bill?

BILL. Yes, Darling.

RACHEL. Look into my eyes and answer this one question.

BILL. What's that?

RACHEL. *(As they stare at each other.)* Why are yours so red?

BILL. Is that the question?

RACHEL. No, it's not! The question is—did you spend last night with this woman?

BILL. This woman?

RACHEL. Yes.

BILL. Certainly not.

JULIE. Whew!

RACHEL. You swear?

BILL. Cross my heart.

JULIE. There you are, you see.

RACHEL. *(Puzzled.)* Well, I don't understand. In that case why would Tom say such a thing?

BILL. *(Taking the brush from her.)* How could you think such a thing?

RACHEL. Because Tom said it.

BILL. How could Tom think such a thing?

RACHEL. That's what I want to know.

JULIE. *(To BILL.)* That's what we'd all like to know.

BILL. Shhh!

RACHEL. Why, on the morning of my wedding day, would Tom say such a dreadful thing about his best friend?

JULIE. He's distraught.

RACHEL. Why?

JULIE. Because I turned him down.

RACHEL. But what about the other one.

BILL. What other one?

RACHEL. The other girlfriend.

BILL. Um... *(Confidentially, indicating JULIE.)* She's not supposed to know about the other one.

RACHEL. Why shouldn't she know about the other one? She's turned him down now.

JULIE. That's all right, I do know about the other one.

RACHEL. Do you?

JULIE. Yes. That's why I turned him down.

RACHEL. Ah. That's all right then. So what happened to her?

JULIE. She turned him down as well.

RACHEL. Did she?

JULIE. *(To BILL.)* Didn't she?

BILL. Yes.

JULIE. Which is why he's so distraught.

BILL. *(Aside.)* That's good.

JULIE. Thank you.

RACHEL. I see.

JULIE. Right then. If that's everything, I'll get on and leave you two to get on with getting married... if you're sure you get on enough to *want* to get married.

(JULIE beams brightly, and leaves.)

RACHEL. What did she mean by that?

BILL. Haven't the foggiest.

RACHEL. You do want to get married, don't you, Bill?

BILL. Of course.

RACHEL. I must say, you don't look as if you do.

BILL. Don't I?

RACHEL. *(Looking at her watch.)* There's less than a quarter of an hour to go... *(Looks out of the window.)* everyone is piling into the church... and here you are, a total wreck, and behaving as if you're going to your own execution!

BILL. It's nerves.

RACHEL. Nerves?

BILL. All men get nerves on their wedding day.

RACHEL. Your nerves look like a nervous breakdown. I'm not marrying a wimp, am I Bill? I'd hate to feel I was the strong one in this marriage.

BILL. So would I.

RACHEL. What?

BILL. I mean, I'd hate to feel the weak one.

RACHEL. Right—well prove you're not by getting yourself down the aisle in one piece, will you?

BILL. Right.

RACHEL. You may kiss me for the last time as your fiancee. *(BILL goes to kiss her.)* But don't smudge my make-up.

(BILL kisses RACHEL on the cheek. She goes into the bedroom, as JUDY comes out of the bathroom, fully dressed again. BILL puts down the toilet brush and goes to stare disconsolately out of the window.)

BILL. Oh God!

RACHEL. *(To JUDY.)* Oh. You're still here.

JUDY. I'm just leaving. I'm going back to London.

RACHEL. That's probably wise.

JUDY. I'm sorry to have been so much in the way.

RACHEL. I'm sorry this weekend hasn't worked out for you.

JUDY. Yes.

RACHEL. Say good-bye to Bill. He's next door.

JUDY. Er ... right.

(JUDY goes through to the reception room. RACHEL sits at the dressing table to finish her hair.)

JUDY. Good-bye, Bill.

BILL. *(Turning.)* Judy.

JUDY. I'm just leaving.

BILL. Where to?

JUDY. Back to London.

BILL. Oh, Judy.

JUDY. I'm sorry we didn't meet a year ago.

BILL. So'm I.

JUDY. I'll never forget last night.

BILL. Neither will I.

JUDY. But I'm sure you and Rachel will be very happy.

BILL. *(Very unhappily.)* Oh God...

JUDY. *(Holding out her hand.)* Good-bye.

(BILL takes her hand. They hesitate. Then can't prevent themselves kissing. In the middle of the embrace TOM enters.)

TOM. Aha!

BILL. Oh, my God!

TOM. I *knew* that was it!

BILL. Now, Tom...

JUDY. I was just going, Tom.

TOM. Where? Back to bed? *(Goes for BILL.)* I'm going to kill you!

BILL. *(Dodging him.)* No, Tom, no...

JUDY. No, no... *(TOM catches BILL and throttles him on the sofa.)* Stop!

(A panting DAPHNE enters from the passage, her outfit and hat awry.)

DAPHNE. Stop!

(RACHEL hears the noise and enters from the bedroom.)

RACHEL. Stop!

TOM. *(Still throttling.)* I'll stop when he's stopped breathing!

BILL. Ggggg!

(JULIE enters. She takes in the scene, and issues an ear-splitting whistle. The brawl ceases.)

JULIE. Right—that's it! That's the final straw! I've had my bellyful of you lot! This entire hotel's collapsing around my ears because of you maniacs, and I'm getting the blame for it! I've never met such a bunch in my life! Comparing you to rabbits is an insult to rabbits! Last night nobody knew which beds they slept in—nobody knew which people they slept with—nobody knew which day it was! This morning they've realized what day it is and they've turned from rabbits into headless chickens! They're squawking in the lobby, they're flapping in the restaurant, they're fighting in the bedrooms!

RACHEL. Now just a minute...

JULIE. There are people chasing people round the corridors, there are people trying to kill people with carving knives, there are people strangling people on the furniture!

DAPHNE. Just a minute...

JULIE. Meanwhile our receptionist has resigned because she's told the rooms are all mixed up, our head waiter's resigned because he's told the tables are all mixed up, our night porter's resigned because he's told his call girls are all mixed up. On top of which, I've been given the sack because I'm mixed up with your bloody mix-up!

RACHEL. *(Puzzled.)* The sack?

JULIE. *(Going to the door.)* Well my final duty is to tell you from the manager that as far as he's concerned you can all go and get married somewhere else—you're not doing it in *this* hotel!

(JULIE opens the door and waves them all out.)

DAPHNE. He can't throw us out now. The service is just about to start!

JULIE. How can it start? Look at you all! *(Indicates BILL.)* The bridegroom looks as if he's been in a football scrum. *(Indicates TOM.)* The best man looks as if he's escaped from a padded cell. *(Indicates DAPHNE.)* The bride's mother looks as if she's out of a pantomime...

DAPHNE. Oh!

JULIE. *(Pointing downstairs.)* And the bride's father looks as if he's out of a zoo!

DAPHNE. How dare you!

JULIE. He's been thrown out of the hotel, and banned from ever coming back!

DAPHNE. *(Rushing to the window.)* Oh, poor Gerald!

JULIE. And I've been told to tell you, that goes for the rest of you too.

RACHEL. I don't understand. What have you got to do with all this?

JULIE. Far too much!

RACHEL. You're one of Tom's girlfriends.

JULIE. I'm not anybody's girlfriend—least of all his.

RACHEL. What are you then?

BILL. Julie...
JULIE. I'm a chambermaid!
BILL. Oh God!
RACHEL. A chambermaid?
JULIE. Yes.
RACHEL. *(Indicating JUDY.)* And who's this?
JULIE. She's everybody's girlfriend.
JUDY. Oh God!
RACHEL. Is this true, Julie?
JULIE. Judy.
RACHEL. What?
JULIE. That's Judy. I'm Julie.

(Pause. RACHEL takes a deep breath and draws herself to full height.)

RACHEL. Right. No more lies, no more stories, no more excuses. I want to know just what the hell has been going on here.
DAPHNE. *(At the window.)* The wedding's due to start at any moment, Rachel. I can see your father at the church door, shouting at the vicar!
RACHEL. The wedding will have to wait, Mother. I am not going down that aisle until someone tells me the truth.
JULIE. About time.
RACHEL. Well, Tom?
TOM. *(Indicating BILL.)* Ask him!
RACHEL. Well, Bill?
BILL. I don't know what the truth is any more.
RACHEL. *Well* somebody?
JUDY. I think I'd better tell you.
TOM. Good idea.
RACHEL. Thank you, Julie.
JUDY. Judy.
RACHEL. Julie, Judy—I don't care what your name is—just tell me the truth!

JUDY. The truth is... that I spent last night with Bill... *(Pointing.)* in that bedroom... in that bed.

TOM. Hah!

DAPHNE. *(Aghast.)* Ohhh!

BILL. *(Despairing.)* Ohhh.

RACHEL. *(Cold.)* Oh.

JUDY. It just came about by accident—because we were both drunk, and in a bit of a state, and couldn't find which rooms we were meant to be in, and... we somehow ended up in the same one.

DAPHNE. Ohhhh!

TOM. Hah!

RACHEL. Ah.

JUDY. However...

DAPHNE. What?

TOM. What?

JUDY. You may not believe this...

RACHEL. What?

JUDY. But nothing actually happened between us.

RACHEL. Oh?

TOM. Oh?

JUDY. Bill was concussed, and so drunk he can't even remember much about it. Can you, Bill?

BILL. No.

JUDY. And I... well, however much I may have wanted something to happen... it didn't because Bill was getting married.

RACHEL. Considerate of you.

JUDY. And although he's in a complete fog about it... it was his decision as much as mine.

RACHEL. Was it, Bill?

BILL. I, er...

JUDY. Yes it was. We thought we could save the situation, and pretend it didn't happen—but in the end we couldn't— the confusion just got worse and worse—which is why I'm telling you.

RACHEL. I see.

JUDY. That's all there is to it. So now there's really nothing to stop you getting on with your wedding.

TOM. Hold on a minute.

JUDY. What?

RACHEL. What?

TOM. *(To JUDY.)* You're telling us nothing happened?

JUDY. Yes.

TOM. It was a chance encounter that didn't mean anything?

JUDY. Yes.

TOM. Then in that case...

JUDY. What?

TOM. Why did you tell me it was the biggest moment of your life?

RACHEL. Did she?

TOM. And why has Bill been acting as if today is the biggest disaster of his life?

RACHEL. Has he?

TOM. And last but not least, why was he kissing you when I came into the room just now?

(Pause.)

RACHEL. Was he?

TOM. Yes!

RACHEL. *(Turning to BILL.)* Were you, Bill?

BILL. Er... well... I...

RACHEL. *(Turning to JUDY.)* Was he, Judy?

JUDY. No.

TOM. I saw you!

JUDY. I was kissing him.

RACHEL. Why?

JUDY. Because...

RACHEL. Well?

JUDY. Because... all right, I love him.

(Collective intake of breath.)

BILL. Oh, Judy...
TOM. I knew it!

(RACHEL turns slowly to BILL.)

RACHEL. Bill?
BILL. Yes, Rachel.
RACHEL. Why were you letting Judy kiss you?
BILL. Because...
RACHEL. Well?
DAPHNE. Well?
TOM. Well?
BILL. Because I love her.

(Bigger collective intake of breath. Small squeak from DAPHNE.)

JUDY. Oh, Bill...
RACHEL. Oh, Mummy...

(RACHEL half faints. TOM catches her. He carries her to the sofa and kneels beside her. DAPHNE comes to her other side.)

DAPHNE. Oh, my poor darling... Our perfect wedding...
BILL. I'm sorry, Rachel.
DAPHNE. Men! They're all the same.
BILL. But if you think about it we never were really right for each other.
RACHEL. Ohhhh...

(The sound of a single church bell is heard through the window. DAPHNE gasps.)

DAPHNE. It's time for the service! What are we going to do?

RACHEL. *(Weakly.)* I don't know.

DAPHNE. Are you *sure* there's no-one else you'd like to marry?

(Pause. TOM takes RACHEL's hand.)

TOM. I'll marry you if you like, Rachel.

(Even bigger collective intake.)

DAPHNE. Tom?
BILL. Tom?
RACHEL. Tom?
TOM. I've always wanted to.

(Pause.)

RACHEL. *(Astounded.)* Tom?
TOM. You were always tied to Bill. I couldn't tell you.
RACHEL. *(In wonder.)* Tom... ?
TOM. It's why I've never found anyone else.
RACHEL. *(Gratified.)* Tom!

(RACHEL bursts into tears and flings her arms round TOM.)

TOM. If you think about it I *am* rather right for you.
RACHEL. Oh, thank you, thank you, Tom!
DAPHNE. *(With feeling.)* Yes, thank you, Tom.

(Cheers and applause from everyone. JULIE picks up the toilet brush and takes charge again.)

JULIE. Thank heavens for that! *(Waving the brush.)* Right, that's settled—off to the church you lot. You can all get married to each other, and let the hotel get back to business!
BILL. Here now, wait a minute...

JUDY. Yes, wait a minute...

JULIE. What's the matter?

BILL. We didn't mean... Judy and I can't...

JULIE. What's the problem? You love each other. The church is waiting. Get on with it.

BILL. Yes, but we...

JUDY. We hardly know each other...

JULIE. You should have thought of that before you hopped into bed together. Rabbits! *(Waves the brush.)* Off you all go, please! *(Pushes BILL.)* Out! Everybody out!

BILL. Just a minute...

JULIE. *(Pushing JUDY.)* Out!

JUDY. Just a minute...

JULIE. *(Pushing TOM.)* Out!

TOM. Here, who are you shoving?

JULIE. *(Herding DAPHNE and RACHEL as well.)* Out, out! Everybody leaves now, or we're calling the police!

RACHEL. Don't you push us around!

DAPHNE. You're just a chambermaid!

(They all struggle with JULIE. BILL attracts JUDY's attention, and together they sidle past the others towards the connecting door.)

JULIE. *(Pushing.)* Out! Out!

RACHEL. Here, don't you hit my fiance!

(Thumps JULIE.)

JULIE. Out!

(Swipes RACHEL with the brush.)

DAPHNE. Here, don't you hit my daughter!

(Thumps JULIE with her handbag. The four are locked in a struggling mass. BILL and JUDY close the connecting door, and are alone in the bedroom. BILL pulls the air tickets from his back picket.)

BILL. Do you fancy a holiday in Jamaica?
JUDY. Yes, please!

(They slip out of the bedroom, as the struggle in the next room develops into a riot, and the church bells break into a demanding peal.)

END OF PLAY

COSTUME PLOT

BILL
Bikini Underwear
Boxer Shorts
Tan Khaki Slacks
Blue Button-down Shirt
Tan Lace-up Shoes
Tan Socks
White Tuxedo Shirt
Starched White Collar
Black Bow Tie
Black Tuxedo Pants
Black Wedding Shoes
Black Socks

JUDY
Strapless Beige Bra
Beige Underwear
White Bra
Nylons
Full White Slip
Fitted Yellow Dress
Yellow Belt
Pearl Necklace
Pearl Earrings

TOM
Black Tuxedo
White Tuxedo Shirt
Forest Green Cummerbund
Forest Green Bow Tie
Gold Cuff-links
Black Wedding Shoes
Black Socks

RACHEL
Red Tailored Dress suit
Matching Red Hat
Red High Heeled Shoes
White Day Gloves
Full White Slip
Nylons
Pink Silk Bathrobe
Matching High Heeled Slippers
Wedding Dress (also fit Judy)
White Petticoat
White Stockings
White Wedding Shoes

JULIE
Striped Short Sleeved Shirt
Bright Orange Shorts
Orange Tennis Shoes
White Anklets
Gold Necklace and Earrings
Forest Green Cover-all Apron

DAPHNE
Violet Dress: Black Silk trim
Matching Hat with Feathers
Black Hand Bag
Black High Heeled Shoes
Nylons

PROPERTIES LIST

Room Service Tray - with used breakfast dishes
Two Telephones - to match Country House Hotel furnishings
Bed Made with - bottom sheet, top sheet and two pillowcases
Two Bed Pillows
Throw Pillows
Bedspread
Toilet Brush - with wooden handle
Two Airline Tickets
Stack of Good Luck Messages
Glass of Alka Seltzer
Small Suitcase
Large Carry-all (or Purse) containing:
        Blank Note Cards with Pen
        Vanity Case with:
           Manicure set
           Make-up bag
           Hairbrush
           Bobbypins
Set of Hotel Keys
Complete Extra Bed Set: Two Sheets and Pillowcases
Large Clear Plastic Garment Bag
Sewing Basket containing:
        Pin Cushion
        Scissors
        Needles
        Thread
Cake Knife
Bird Feathers

FURNITURE
Reception Room:
    Small Message Table
    Desk with Chair
    Chaise Lounge
Bedroom:
    Vanity Table and Chair
    Double Bed
    Tray Jack
    Armchair
    Pouf

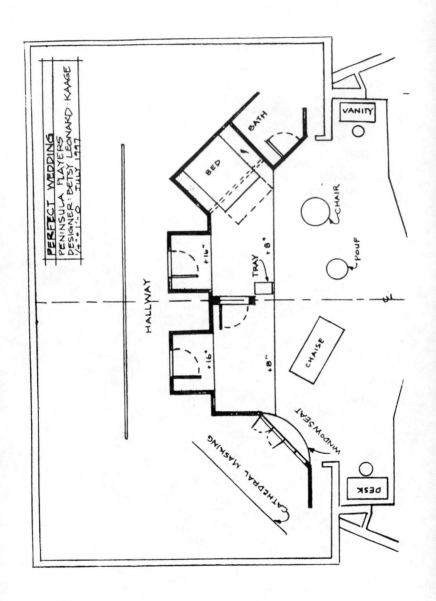